# Retribution Guns

# Retribution Guns

VIC J. HANSON

**A Black Horse Western**

ROBERT HALE · LONDON

© Vic J. Hanson 2000
First published in Great Britain 2000

ISBN 0 7090 6770 4

Robert Hale Limited
Clerkenwell House
Clerkenwell Green
London EC1R 0HT

Typeset by
Derek Doyle & Associates, Liverpool.
Printed and bound in Great Britain by
The Cromwell Press

*For Sue, Keith and the Girls*

# Part One

# WILD TARGETS

# Introduction

Daliol was the first and he was easy: they hoped the others would be as easy. They had not had to search for Daliol. A range detective who was no killer had been the first on the trail, had found out about the new name the man was using and where he had settled in order to make a fresh life for himself.

Sitting pretty. But that was soon changed.

Daliol was the eldest. He had been the leader. It was fitting that he should be the first.

As usual, they flipped a coin. The one who won chose a rifle. With an old bastard like Daliol a stand-up gunfight would have been inappropriate anyway.

Every morning he went riding out of town. And there were convenient bluffs which he reached before turning back. The rifleman was steady, swift, expert. Two shots, the second as the man was driven from the saddle. Then he lay, did not move again, looked for all the world like a heap of rags tossed away in the middle of the dusty trail under the sun.

There was nobody else in sight. They had made sure

of that, did so again before quitting the bluffs and riding away. Nobody came after them.

The detective, an ex-Pinkerton, had long gone. They hadn't even met him: there'd been a go-between. And a 'principal' before that: the hirer, the money-man. They didn't know who he was either, didn't want to know him (or her) any more than that person would want to know them. They were professional, went for what they were after, no more than that. Then they rested for a while: they had ways. What they were getting for this job was the richest ever.

The rest of it would not be as easy, though, not like old Daliol. The detective knew names but had not got much else. He was out now, and they, the two of them, were still in Kansas but figured they would have to go over the border for the next one. Even further maybe as, after hiding their tracks, the other two fugitives had probably separated.

The go-between, a sort of murder broker, had given them a scrawled map which had not been of much use so far, but might be.

It was night when they crossed the old Loving–Goodnight cattle trail, looking bleak and ghostly, empty under a pale moon.

Not so very long after that they were in New Mexico and the sun was blazing like a message from hell.

They had connections all over the place, so had picked up smidgens of information as they rode on their enigmatic way. They asked questions and got answers, some pretty good, others not so. Nobody asked them questions: they weren't the sort you asked questions of. To some folk they were known. Others looked at them warily, these two quiet men with soft voices and few words, no procrastinations. Sometimes *dinero* changed hands, began to do this more in New Mexico where the old word was maybe a leetle more in favour than it was in Kansas.

Santa Fe was mentioned. But they were still a long way away from there. Then a town was mentioned which they had never heard of before. A sort of gambling hideout led by a king-pin. They hadn't heard of the town – but they'd heard of the king-pin.

And one of the men they sought now was an inveterate gambler.

He had demonstrated also that he was quick with a pistol, a well-spoken, smiling killer with slick fingers.

They did not cut the cards this time. One of them was a faster gunhand than the other, with a Colt not a Winchester. It was his turn anyway and he volunteered. Mightn't come to anything yet anyway, the other one said. That slick, elusive bastard could be in Texas now or even over the big river and talking pidgin English with the *señoritas*. They had heard he was pretty good at that also.

Still and all, the luck stayed with them. But they did not think for one moment that this one would be as easy as old Daliol.

The town was called, very appropriately, Ace Hole, and it stood on the slopes of a gentle hill with a narrow

11

creek running at the bottom. The sun was going down and there was nobody else on the narrow well-used trail. They decided to make a detour. They came in on the creek side, letting their horses drink before continuing. Everything looked kind of peaceful. This was no wide-open cowtown, that was for sure. They had not seen any beef for miles. Folks didn't come to this outpost to buy and sell meat on the hoof. Its reputation rested on something else entirely.

'Easy,' they said. '*Easy.*'

A team of two who were very good at what they did, they always took it easy.

A small town but neat and looking kind of prosperous. And an old hostler who said 'Evenin' gents, an' welcome.'

They went first to the bath-house which had a barber's shop incorporated in the long, low, clapboard building. There were two tubs, both of them luckily empty, only to be filled by water from an ingeniously-modified pump with two cunningly bent pipes atached. The hot water was toted from a stove by a hare-lipped youth who went by the name of Rube, who stammered his thanks at the largesse given to him by the two gents.

They both had haircuts and shaves and a fine brushdown, knowing that their horses would be as well looked after by the genial oldster back at the stables.

They were at the other end of town now. The local bordello was only a few doors away and, in the sun, didn't look half bad, having obviously been recently repainted.

The two boys always figured that a whorehouse was the best place to pick up information if you went about it the right way, nice an' easy.

A madam, usually risen from the ranks you might say, was kind of businesslike and could be as tight-mouthed as a fractious old mule with a teeth problem. But her girls, no matter what they had been told, could oftimes prattle like nosy school-kids, particularly to a handsome *caballero* who was well-britched in more ways than a few.

One of the boys went upstairs with a honey-tongued Mexican filly. He took longer than his partner, who had a big German blonde, who, unluckily, didn't have much Americanes. But the other feller came down with his lean face wreathed in smiles and, after they quitted the place, said:

'She knows him, has been with him, says he's mean. And I ain't.'

'I know, bucko, go on.'

'He calls himself Dingo now, but she knows his real name, the one we'd got. He plays cards every night down at the saloon called The Wideawake, which is open all hours.'

'Where'd you figure he'll be late tonight, last thing altogether. Down at the saloon or the other place?'

'The saloon. The *señorita* thinks he's been losing some lately.'

'How do you want to play this then?'

'I'll think o' somep'n.'

Separately, they entered The Wideawake, a spacious, busy well-run place. They spotted their man, signalled to each other by a scratch on the nose. They left separately, conferred in a nearby alley then drifted apart once more.

It was late when their quarry left the saloon, shouting good-night to two cronies who went in different directions. He was singing softly to himself. Maybe he had been making up his losses.

He had a room in a nearby boarding-house. They followed him at a discreet distance, then one took the front, the other the back.

He visited one of the three privies outback, and by then the house was in darkness.

The two partners rejoined each other and the one from the back said:

'I guess I know how to do it now. If he's a creature of habit that is. I reckon that.'

The following day they did not go around town together, even fed in different places. Late that night the shooter was at his post waiting. He caught the fancy sharper coming out of the privy and softly spoke his name. His real name. Which seemed to surprise the feller.

'Who are you? What do you want?'

'I hear you're fast with a gun. I'll give you a chance to draw. If you don't take that chance I'm gonna kill you anyway and take your poke.'

'A goddam robber!' the fancy man snarled. His hand dipped. But he was outclassed. He took the slug full in the chest.

The other man sheathed his weapon. He bent over

14

the body and could not detect any signs of life. He dragged the body into the privy, kicking the fallen weapon in after it, and shut the door as tightly as he could.

He had done what he had had to do. He didn't want the man's damn' poke.

His partner was nowhere around, was on his way back to the false-front hotel where they were both staying, in separate rooms. They didn't meet till the following morning and that was after breakfast – they weren't supposed to know each other – mingling with the crowd in the saloon when the mysterious killing was being talked about. An early riser had found 'it' propped up in the privy like a praying idol. The old-timer had almost had a heart attack.

Everybody was talking. Yammering faces, many of them not known to anybody else. Folks came and went. Hell, this was a gamblin' town!

But the dead man had not even been robbed. He had made a killing at the table last night, somebody said. Others chortled – yeh, in more ways than one.

Out of the corner of his mouth a certain well-set-up young man said to another feller of a like stripe, 'You had to do it your way, didn't you? Fancy!'

'Yeh. I did it clean, didn't I?'

'He could've been faster than you.'

'He wasn't.'

'Maybe he was drunk.'

'Nah, he was a fast-fingered cardsharp, not a boozer. Let's get outa here.'

They left separately. They had learned there was no actual law in Ace Hole. The gambling fraternity sort of policed themselves. The king-pin, who actually owned The Wideawake, was called Long Perce. He wasn't going to bother his head much about a fancy drifter who had gotten himself bushwhacked.

Acting on information, the two partners went after their third man. They figured their luck was still with them and this one might turn out to be another easy one.

A youngish, dark-skinned jasper with a V-shaped scar on his right cheek.

They caught up with him; but maybe they acted a mite too eager or something. The man lit out and they went after him. Hell, they were right on his tail!

'*I* can take 'im,' the rifleman said. And he did too.

A bullet in the back of the head – and a scarred face in the dust.

It was not so long afterwards however that the two partners learned that, scar or no scar, they had got the wrong man.

Furthermore, they were not to collect the rest of the *dinero* which would be due to them. They had to get the right target: their reputation rested on that.

# ONE

Deputy Gallaghan was mighty glad the town was in sight at last. He'd bet his prisoner was all-fired glad too; he certainly had a right to be.

The heat of the sun was blistering, despite the fact that they both had their wideawake hats pulled down over their eyes. In fact, the prisoner, name of Daley Clegg, was slumped forward over the neck of his horse; though Gallaghan couldn't make himself feel sorry for the vicious little bastard.

Daley had his hands lashed together at the wrists, but not cruelly, could still hold his reins. He had a swollen ankle which he had gotten in stumbling up a hill away from the deputy after his horse had been shot from under him. Damn' bad shooting Gallaghan had called it, though his own horse had stumbled on rough ground, spoiling its rider's aim. And the other poor beast, shot in the back of the head, had paid for that.

While the disarmed Daley had squatted on the sloping, rocky ground, cursing, nursing his twisted ankle,

17

Gallaghan had covered the horse's body with rocks, not wanting him to have the final indignity of becoming buzzard bait.

He had been a fine beast. Daley had picked the best of a stable back in town after he had shot a rich gambler in the back and taken his poke.

The town shimmering in a heat haze. But it was the right place all right. Daley should have been dragged along there at the end of a rope, Gallaghan reflected. But, knowing that Daley had stolen a fine mount, the deputy had taken a spare horse along, so the back-shooting killer, busted ankle or not, was so far getting better treatment than he deserved.

Gallaghan's chief, Sheriff Trig Bestor was laid up with croup. He had another sort of deputy besides Lem, an old mossyhorn with a twisted leg who was more of a jailer and swamper than anything else, working at the local rathskellar as well.

It was a long time since they had had a killer in a cell, one of two in back of the jail office. Particularly a back-shooting scumhound like Daley Clegg who had been skulking around town for some time.

Lem Gallaghan had said he could handle Daley. Besides, the young man that Daley had killed in a bush-whack by night had been a friend of the deputy's.

Gallaghan had kept an unspoken promise to a dead *amigo*; and there was Daley, ahead of the deputy, proving it.

Folks rode out to meet them. A few ran in the background. There were threatening shouts.

18

'He's my prisoner,' Gallaghan said. 'He's going behind bars.'

Nobody bucked him then. But he had an escort which became quite a crowd, before the jail-office door closed on him and his prisoner.

The local sawbones arrived to look at Daley's ankle, though the consensus was that it should have been his neck.

Gradually the mob outside the jail dispersed.

The doc looked at Daley's ankle, salved it, bandaged it, took his leave.

Gallaghan went into the sheriff who still lay in bed in the big room next to the jailhouse kitchen.

'So you got 'im.'

''Pears like it, don't it?'

Still, the older man's brow was clouded and his next words proved that this wasn't due to the fact that just maybe his present condition was bothering him.

'I've had some bad news, Lem. Telegraph.'

'Oh, what about?'

'God, I'm sure mighty sorry to have to tell you this. Your friend, Christopher Dakes, is dead. Bushwhacked.'

Gallaghan did not say anything right off, just stared at Trig Bestor. He was normally quite a poker-faced young man. But the grief grew slowly in his eyes. Then he said:

'Where?'

'Place called Baker's Dip. In New Mexico.'

'I know it. Anybody caught?'

'Not yet it seems. No clues I guess. Nothing.'

19

'Bounty-hunters?'

'Who knows? Hell, Lem, the price has been taken off Christopher's head long since. It's been proved he had nothing to do with the killing he was blamed for. All the dodgers have been called in. I destroyed some right here, you know that.'

'Sure, I know.'

'I guess there might be some tattered ones hanging about, pinned up an' fallin' to pieces up-country. But if bounty-hunters did what happened to Christopher they were damn' amateurs, weren't they? They can't get anything out of it, can they?'

'Somebody Christopher upset maybe. Somehow. Though he was kind of keepin' his head way down.'

'I guess you knew where he was.'

'I did. Staying with his widowed sister in Baker's Dip, her and her boy – his only nephew and him mighty fond of the sprig. Helpin' with the farm. Julie's man was kicked to death by a wild horse.'

'I remember you tol' me about that.'

'Guess I did at that . . . I've got to go see, Trig.'

'I know, boy. I'll soon be outa this damn' bed. I'll get somebody to cover for you for a while. Young Prince for instance . . .'

'He'll jump at it. I think he'd be all right, though . . .' Gallaghan paused. Then he said, haltingly. 'No mistake, huh?'

'I don't imagine so, son. Scar an' all. I think it was Christopher all right.'

'No two like him in that town I guess,' said

Gallaghan. He turned slowly, opened the door, went out.

Brackley was fat and oily. He called himself a lawyer but all he was was a chancer, a broker, an agent, a crooked go-between.

He looked up at the two young men who stood at the other side of his handsome mahogany desk and he said:

'I swear – I didn't know.'

'It's your job to make sure.'

'I got in touch with you right away.'

'That was afterwards.'

Although the two young men looked like brothers and seemed to share pretty well everything right down the middle – as far as Brackley knew anyway – it was always the same one who did the talking. Maybe the older one: it was difficult to figure. The other one only murmured a little from time to time, and the rest of the time he watched. Oh, how he *watched*! With pale killer's eyes. And a tenseness about him, a sureness that was palpable and terrifying, making Brackley sweat more than he usually did.

'It was that range detective, huh, he gave you the information?'

The fat man licked dry lips. 'Yes.'

'Anything else? Since.'

'He's working on it.'

'Where is he?'

'I wasn't supposed to tell you that. He doesn't know who you are. You know how I work.'

21

'Tell us,' said the one who did not usually talk much.

His partner jerked a thumb. 'You better tell us, or my friend is gonna get real mad. He'll hurt you. He might even kill you.'

They still need me, Brackley told himself. But he knew in his heart he could not bank on that. They were so young! So implacable! He had chosen them because they were the best at what they did, but now he wished he had never set eyes on them. I'm tired, he thought.

'I'll tell you,' he said.

# TWO

It would maybe have been better for the two killers in the long run if they had shut fat Brackley's mouth for good when they had the chance. Then they might also have gone on to the so-called range detective whose name they now knew, and also his approximate whereabouts.

Not long after the visit of the disgruntled young men, Brackley received another visitor of much the same stripe, even the same age give or take a year or so.

'Lem Gallaghan,' he said. 'By all that's holy.' He beamed. But his oily smile did not reach his piggy eyes, which had cunning in them, if a modicum of an uncertain fear also.

'You're still on the old game, huh?' Gallaghan said.

'Well, I'm not as young as I used to be, Lem, and I'm not exactly a well man. I have to make a living as best I can.'

'The old way?'

'It depends on what you want, Lem. It depends on

why you're here to see me. I thought you were a lawman now.'

'I am. But I have other interests right now.'

'As I remember you always did have other interests. Er–um, when it suited your book.'

'Still the double-talk,' Gallaghan said. 'Always the double-talk.'

'It is the Spanish way, *amigo*.'

But suddenly the other man's eyes were blazing. 'I figured you. An' I've found you. And I want to ask you some questions. Hell, you're no Spaniard.'

'Ask your questions. I have always been your friend. You needed me once.'

'You helped me. You had your reasons, by Gar you did. And that was a long time ago.' No more double-talk from Gallaghan, at least. 'You as a go-between hired two killers to do a job. But they didn't do the job properly. I want the names of those two and I want to know where they are.'

'How did you. . .?'

'Never mind that. Names!'

'They'd kill me.'

'I'd kill you before they could. You know I could do that.'

'You can't handle them, Lem. They—'

'Names!' And now the tall young man was bending over the desk, his grey-blue eyes steely. And he had a Colt Lightning in his fist, pointing straight at Brackley's sweat-bedewed brow.

The fat man slumped back into his chair. 'I'll tell you

24

what I can. I don't know names, though. They don't use names.'

'You'll tell!' said Gallaghan. 'Make sure of that. Squeeze it. Talk!'

He did not imagine for a moment that Brackley would do just that, but he aimed to squeeze as much juice out of the man as he possibly could. He sheathed his gun, drew a chair closer to him, sat down upon it.

Brackley talked in a wheezy voice, sweating profusely all the time. The sweating was natural, but the wheezy voice didn't fool the listener. The man wasn't sick, just scared for his own blubbery skin. Gallaghan wondered whether Brackley kept a pistol in the drawer of his desk like he used to . . . . But surely he wouldn't try and reach for it. He knew Gallaghan was fast. Faster now maybe than he had ever been.

The fat man quit talking. He looked drained, but maybe that was probably pretty much of a put-on thing.

'This range detective,' said Gallaghan. 'Where's he at now?'

'The two boys might have got there first.'

'Tell me anyway.'

Brackley told him, added, 'As far as I know.'

'The buyer?' said Gallaghan.

'I've told you, Lem, like I keep telling you, I don't know. He gave his name is all. Obviously an alias. An important man. A rich elderly man using an obvious alias. He made no secret of that. A rich job. But, Jehosophat, I wish now I'd never heard of it.'

'Horse-shit,' said Gallaghan as he rose.

He walked round the desk. Brackley flinched. The tall man leaned over him, pulled open the drawer and yanked out the Smith and Wesson pistol.

'You never change, do you?'

'Neither do you,' said Brackley, knowing that he was not yet to be shot.

'I've changed,' said Gallaghan. 'I'm just gonna do somep'n that I have to do, that's all.'

He tucked the neat pearl-handled gun in the back of his belt, skirted the desk again, made for the door. Over his shoulder he said:

'Keep your mouth shut. About me. About everything.'

'I will.'

It was a short and hollow phrase.

He had known that even if he travelled there right from his home ground and rode hard he would not be in time for the funeral. The heat was intense and the ground was hard and he had at least one thing to do before he made for Baker's Dip and Julie and her boy and the place where Christopher had been shot down like a useless cur-dog.

At first he had been overcome by an almost uncontrollable fury. He had felt like it was sometimes in the old days when he was a wild boy running with wild company, although deep down he hadn't liked feeling that way. He could have turned on other people like some folks did, used a 'whipping boy'.

But who could he have turned on back in that town

26

he had been so glad to call his home; Sheriff Trig Bestor? His old deputy? The prisoner, Daley Clegg? Hell, Daley was a whipping boy already and richly deserved to be: he would get *his* come-uppance!

Fat Brackley had served the bill, though. The villain had been scoured *scared*, had believed Gallaghan's blood-curdling threats – for Brackley had known the old Gallaghan.

Gallaghan had an implacable resolve. But it was a quiet thing now. There was no fury in it, no hate. You couldn't have shadows.

Not until they became reality – and then you could deal with them in the way you had to.

It was like being in the old days. But not exactly like that; and there was the mercy.

He told himself that it had all been a long time ago. He was not yet thirty, however. He had tried to forget the old times, put them behind him for ever. But he couldn't have forgotten Christopher. As he got nearer to his destination he remembered Christopher more and more, wished he had been there to save him from what had happened as Christopher had once saved him, Gallaghan, and got that terrible scar in the doing.

And there had been Julie. How could he possibly have forgotten Julie?

He hadn't. No! There had been others, too many of them maybe; he was a big, handsome cuss: women had told him so.

But he had to admit now, should've admitted it before: he could never forget Julie.

27

It was like a dream – as he dozed in the saddle under the hot sun, the horse carrying him forward . . . .

And then she was suddenly there, coming out on the stoop, shading her eyes with her hand to see who the approaching rider might be. He saw the glint of the rifle which leaned against the post within arm's reach to the right of her. She was a staunch frontier lady who had lately lost a beloved brother in the worst possible way, and she was wary, suddenly *ready*.

But then she left the stoop and, as she came down the steps, he knew she had recognized him.

She raised her arms and then held them out as she broke into a run.

He saw the tears in her eyes, and the grief, and the love; and he reined in his mount. He slid down from the saddle and moved towards her, his step quickening.

# THREE

They rode hard. It was possible that both of them figured they had done too much riding of late, but neither of them passed an opinion about that. They could have taken a train. But neither of them were keen on trains. You could be spotted on trains. Folks might remember you and in their line of business that wouldn't do at all.

When they got to their destination they took a bath. They shaved. One of them needed a new shirt. He got one.

They had a few drinks and a frugal meal in a local saloon. At separate tables. So that nobody would know they were together. Not that anybody seemed to notice anything much anyway. This was a quiet town, a respectable town. They could understand why the man they sought had chosen it for his billet.

Not till they got to the rooming-house did they get together, figuring they would be leaving right afterwards anyway.

The landlady was lean, rawboned, hatchet-featured. Certainly no fashion plate. Reminding him, one of the boys said, of a sergeant-major he'd onec known, adding, 'I gave him his come-uppance, though.'

'I'll just bet you did,' said his partner.

The landlady said, Yeh, of course she knew the feller they'd asked about but that he'd left a few days ago. No, she didn't know where he'd gone. Back East, she thought maybe, where he'd come from in the first place. He'd been a quiet one: she couldn't tell them a thing about him.

They were charming, these two, in a very masculine way. She began to behave as if she was warming to them: a sight to see.

They asked if she could put them up for the night. Even in the room their friend had left if it was still unoccupied: they didn't mind sharing the place.

That was all right. That was arranged. She was a widow, liked men around her.

'You're well in there, boy,' said one to the other. The other one was just a mite younger, and he said, 'I'd rather eat molasses an' broken glass.'

This brought a few guffaws. But by that time they were up in the room. They did it over well but did not find a thing. Still and all, it had been preened up since the feller had left. The place was clean, tidy. The landlady, although she looked like a paleface drugstore Indian, was prim, and severe with it, though good with business no doubt.

In the morning they questioned her again. No, he

hadn't left a thing behind, that one. She hadn't even known what his business was though he had been away from time to time at intervals of various lengths. She was sure he wouldn't be back this time however – he'd purely said so. Yeh, maybe he'd been a drummer of sorts. But she'd never seen him with any sample-cases.

She said she could get a good breakfast done for them. They exchanged glances, and then one of them said 'Thank you very much, ma'am, but we reckon we ought to get going, ain't no use in hanging about now we've missed our friend. We've got other business to attend to, pronto.'

They got some tucker fixed for them at a stores and went on their way and, as they rode, one said, 'I told you in the first place we shouldn't have bothered to come here.'

'So you did. But any time I figure you know every-thin' that is to know I'll part company with yuh an' buy a mule. Anyway, maybe Brackley pulled a fast 'un on us. Maybe he knew all along that that goddam detective was gonna light out.'

'Maybe we ought to kill that fat bastard.'

They cogitated on this while the hooves of the rested horses rattled like the cayuses were all-fired raring to go, *wherever*. No doubt their riders would think of something sooner or later.

They hadn't completely missed anything yet. Only almost . . . .

Back in New Mexico, from a crippled ex-owlhooter the

younger one had known as kid, they got some news. Through the grapevine, he said, which could have been a string of smoke signals for all they knew. Their contact, sitting in a wheelchair, sometimes dispensing advice, picked up all kinds of news items, some just gossip, some not.

The news was of a small bunch that had stuck up a train and gotten away with some bullion. One of them had been wounded by a guard who had himself been killed. Swaying in the saddle, the wounded man had escaped, but his kerchief had slipped down and he'd been spotted. A face easy to remember in that it bore a V-shaped scar. Not an old face. A face similar to the one borne by the jasper that the two professional guns had conspired to murder back by the town of Baker's Dip.

The two boys went a-searching again.

At the rail station where the ambushed train had lighted after the robbery, the two boys accosted a nervous railroad body, passing themselves off as a pair of Pinkertons. The range detective who had eluded them had told fat Brackley the same story and the oily go-between had believed it. Or had pretended to – might've been gospel anyway.

The boys didn't get a hell of a lot of information. But a rumour was going around by now. About a bunch that were supposed to sojourn in the hills near Sonora and a scarfaced man who'd been heading that way.

The boys got away from the station before too many folk managed to see them. They caught no train, nossir. they were as cute as a barrel of monkeys and, by now, as cock-a-hoop as two cowboys who'd scored with half a dozen fillies after a long time on a dusty cattle-trail. Months behind the wagging butts of a slew of beef could make a man thirty for a lot of things.

# FOUR

Folks had not expected to see Deputy Lem Gallaghan leave town again so soon after bringing in the back-shooting prisoner. They waited till night, kept a look-out. Taking turns. Nobody saw Lem return on his big bay called Rip.

Two kids were left on look-out. Other folks, by that time well boozed, drifted down in twos and threes to the jail. The Irish oldster who did watch had limped back to his job of cleaning up the nightspot. He had said that himself was still in bed; the sheriff that is. The office was occupied by a feisty younker called Prince who had done deputying before, an' purely fancied hisself: the old jailer-cum-swamper hadn't relished being bossed around by a snotnosed kid, he said.

The mossyhorn wanted to join in, but they wouldn't let him. He wandered off, mumbling curses under his breath. Soon, after his sweeping and spit-gathering duties were done, he'd grab a free skinful and would forget all about Daley Clegg languishing in the jail waiting to get his neck stretched.

And Daley began to get warning that that dire fate could well befall him long before he expected it.

The mob outside the jail was becoming ever larger and increasingly vocal. Pretty rowdy in fact. And the noise was not at all cheerful. More like the baying of hungry wolves.

And these animals on two legs wanted human flesh: they figured there was only a sick sheriff and a slick-talking younker between them and their prey.

Still and all, whatever you might think about young Prince, you had to admit that he had guts. In hindsight, though, it was a pity that, on that night, Prince's guts and manners slipped over into the foolhardy. Completely alone, he stepped out on to the stoop in front of the jail with a big Colt in each of his fists. He shouted, 'Back off, all o' yuh, or I'll start blasting.'

There was some skittering among the front ranks of the mob. For a split second it might be thought that Prince was going to pull it off. But then, from the back of the mob, where the torches flamed, some drunk threw a bottle which struck the young surrogate deputy on the temple, knocking him back through the half-open door of the jailhouse.

Sheriff Trig Bestor was up and out of his room, fully-dressed, with a shotgun in his fists. With one hand, and coughing all the time, he dragged the unconscious boy further into the office and slammed the door in the faces of the first of the mob-members. He shot the top and bottom bolts.

The door shook as blows were rained upon it. It was

stout, though. The mob would have to get a battering ram.

But there was the back door.

Trig was staggering after his efforts. His eyes were bleary. The room spun around him. He was able to see, however, that without the help of anybody now, Prince was struggling on to his two feet.

'The back door,' croaked Trig. 'We've got to get that bastard out. Nobody's gonna take a prisoner o' mine.'

'Can you. . .?'

'Go on, I'll make it,' snapped Trig.

In the cell Daley Clegg was yelling in a sort of panic. The roars of the mob could be heard out there, and they were blood-curdling, the sound fluctuating like the clamour of a lightning storm. And, if the two lawmen and their prisoner didn't get out of their predicament they might be engulfed by that storm, destroyed by it.

The sheriff, toting his shotgun in one hand, opened the cell-door and shepherded the cursing, wild-eyed prisoner out. The young volunteer deputy, still with his twin Colts, checked through the back door and ascertained that none of the would-be lynchers had thought of it yet.

'Move,' said Sheriff Bestor. 'Loney Dorman's place. I guess they won't think of looking there. We'll figure somep'n.'

He began to cough again, couldn't manage to stop as the three of them made their way along the dark backs of town. The mob was still calling like hungry coyotes.

The two professional killers were pretty sure now that they were hot on the trail of the second scarfaced man, the one they should have taken care of the first time. They had shot the wrong man all right. That didn't bother them at all, except that one of them remarked that it was a pity they couldn't get pay for that job as well, although it had been the wrong job.

They'd put it right now anyway, the other one said, then they'd pick up the full boodle. And maybe a hell of a lot more, if they put the spot on that so-called Pinkerton man.

They had decided to let him simmer for a while anyway because, with the information they now had about the scarfaced owlhooter who billeted in Sonora, to be hot on that trail now was the best bet: that was the way they figured it, agreed upon it.

There was something they didn't know. Although neither of them had claimed he knew everything and, though they joshed each other about this sort of thing, there was certainly something now that they just purely *did not know.*

They did not know that a certain individual called Lem Gallaghan had also gotten information about the scarfaced bandit, and Sonora, and about the two hired killers. And was on their trail!

In their business, they had heard about Lem Gallaghan, though neither of them had ever met him. He'd had a rep that wasn't easy to forget. They didn't know what had happened to him in recent times. They could not dream that he, a noted gunfighter, was dogging them now with vengeance in his heart and two retribution guns in his belt.

# FIVE

A coughing man. A younger man with a spider-trail of blood running from his left temple and down the side of his face. A third man whose age was somewhere midway between the years carried by the other two; and this one a limping man with his hands handcuffed behind his back. Sheriff Trig had not been too bemused to pick up his steel cuffs before he left the jailhouse.

The aforementioned Loney Dorman, who had been a friend of the lawman ever since the latter was a sprig with warlike ambitions, was waiting in cover of darkness outside the back door of his abode, little more than a clapboard-and-wattle soddie, but spacious. It was almost as if he had had a message from the Fates. But he explained, haltingly because he had a pronounced lisp, that he had heard the commotion out front on main street and had wondered what was up.

He was old – not even Trig knew how old Loney was – but he still had all faculties as the sheriff and Deputy

39

Prince well knew, although some folks in town, who were too shortsighted to know any better, still figured the old man who lived in what they thought was some kind of a hole in the ground, was a gibbering moron. To the old man's cackling delight it must be said.

And if Loney could put something across those morons, many of whom would of course be among the would-be lynch mob, he would be delighted to do just that.

The three from the jail had brought three horses with them, led by Prince. His own horse, the sheriff's mount, and another spare one that had been kept, with his two companions, in the tiny corral beside the jail.

Trig had said that if the mob got to the back, as they probably would when some genius gave a thought to that, and found the horses gone, they'd maybe figure that the two lawmen and their captive had lit out for other parts.

The three cayuses munched on straw in a gap-roofed ex-stables near Loney's unconventional abode.

The old man was chuckling like an inebriated loon. It was a tight squeeze in his place – compared to the jail-house anyyway – but Loney said that the trio could stay as long as they liked. This was after he had first, still chuckling, offered to cut the prisoner's throat, a short cut for all of them, would-be hangrope merchants included.

Trig, who at last had quit coughing, said he didn't think Loney's idea was a very good one, and, besides, it wasn't ethical. The prisoner was quiet, sitting with his knees up, leaning lopsided against a muddied wall, awkwardly, his hands manacled behind his back. His eyes were full of hate in the flickering lantern-light as he looked from one to the other and back again, all three. He would like to kill them – and fly away. More than anything, though, he would like to kill the missing gunfighter Lem Gallaghan who had got him into this perilous predicament in the first place.

But these were Gallaghan's friends, goddam their souls to hell!

Big Sheriff Bestor with greying fuzz on his jowly face. Fancy young Prince with his thin moustache and dark eyes. And old Loney, rheumy-eyed and grimacing, who looked like a sack of tied-up rubbish.

And now Loney was going to the narrow doorway which Daley and the others had had to stoop under as they came through. But Loney was a stunted man.

Even so, he blocked the gap, looking out, blocking the light almost completely from the eyes of folks who might be passing by. As a few did right then.

Loney was hiding the escapees. But, it seemed, he wasn't aiming to hide himself. Just the reverse in fact. And a clever ploy when you thought about it.

'What's goin' on, boys? It's kinda noisy down that-away!' His narrow head bobbing like an inquisitive turkey's.

The three men inside couldn't hear the replies, only the sounds of boot-heels.

Loney turned his head, said, 'They're goin' down to see what's happening. But now there's somebody

41

coming from the other direction. Just lie low, boys.'

There didn't seem to be much else they could do. The sheriff was snuffling, didn't look good at all under the yellow light of the hanging lantern.

Loney asked more questions and got answers, turned, still blocking out the light.

'The jailhouse is on fire. The mob busted the door open – an' somebody must've tipped a lamp or somep'n. You boys best get outa 'ere afore somebody spots them three hosses. I'll keep look-out. Then I'll go to the jail an' help out. Some o' the folks 'ull be tryin' to put the fire out 'fore it catches on big. You can bank on that, Trig.'

The sheriff did not say anything, seemed to be having difficulty in getting his breath. Daley Clegg looked at old Loney in amazement.

The crazy coot was actin' like he was a goddamn general or somep'n. Daley hadn't thought much about the old mossyhorn previously. Ol' idiot! But now he was beginning to change his mind, beginning to hate the bossy oldster as much as he hated Bestor and Prince and the missing Gallaghan.

He'd get out of this somehow, like hell he would; and he'd see that these folks got their come-uppances. Nobody messed with Daley Clegg and got away with it, no sir!

They saw the hills back end of Sonora and there was a settlement nearby that seemed to have a large complement of Mexican and *Mestizo* folk who ran various kinds of businesses. The boys figured these people were sort of look-outs and go-betweens and suppliers of grub-stakes and other things. There were some dark *señoritas* around there also and the two partners figured they needed a break. And a *wait*.

One of them said, 'Him who waits, sometimes he prospers, uh?'

'You're full o' shit,' said his friend.

'I know. But somebody might get word. An' somebody might come. I ain't wearing my ass out any more for a while.' A lewd chuckle. 'Not on a hoss anyway.'

They used various aliases. It amused them to think up new ones. Right now the older one – though he wasn't much older than his *amigo*, only bigger – called himself Dougal after a mongrel pooch he'd once owned. The other feller, plumpish, almost boyish, with a pretty, cleft chin to boot, went by the fancy moniker, Armitage, which he claimed to have made up all by himself.

They both figured they were good with the ladies. They vied with each other in their sexual peccadilloes.

Dougal had hard black eyes that could send a shiver down a man's spine. Recently he'd done this with murder broker, Fatty Brackley, there was no denying that.

Women judge men differently from what other men do, though, and Dougal had plenty of takers among the whoredom sorority.

As for Armitage, he could squint his blue orbs like a little kid, and the girls wanted to mother him.

Folks talked to Armitage.

His partner and he met secretly, and the boy said, 'Yeh, most o' the commerce here is run by folks from over the river. But there's all sorts here too. Germans, Swedes, some Chinee – the town drunk is an Englisher. Dutch, Eyetalian, Scots an' Irish, Injuns and Mexes, all kinds an' mixes, you name 'em, they're here. An' all licking an' spittin' an' workin' for an' bargaining with the folks from the hills who are run by a big buck they call Jonesy who's got all kinds in his band as well.'

Dougal laughed brusquely, said, 'You don't know everything, bucko. Down at the place,' he jerked a thumb in the direction of the end of town, 'I had me a filly who never stopped talkin'.'

'Never?'

'I tell you. Never! I heard like you said. But I heard somep'n else. Jonesy's boys usually come in Friday nights. Takin' turns sort of.'

'That's tomorrer.'

'So it is. She knows that scarfaced son-bitch too, though she ain't sure whether he'll come tomorrer night or not.'

'We'll know him if we see him.'

'I hope we surely will this time. An' if he don't come, we'll have to find another way. We can't hang around here too long.'

'All right, I'll fix it,' said Armitage importantly.

Dougal had no rejoinder. They separated again.

# SIX

Gallaghan was a long way from the small ranch now, and he knew where he was going. A kill-trail, he thought, a deadly chain. But he wasn't aiming to get tangled in any damn' *twisted* chain. He was forging steadily onwards.

He hadn't been able to spend long with Julie and her boy, Jonathon, and he was sorry about that. He wanted to get this thing done as soon as possible and get back to lovely Julie; and the boy who had greeted him like a long-lost uncle.

But he wasn't pushing too hard, running too fast, getting too heavy-eyed and butt-cramped. He rode through the night, which was a helluva lot cooler than the day.

He took a break during the day in shade someplace, took some tucker, fed and watered his dun stallion, Rip.

By a creek maybe. And always, if possible, in the shade of a tree. This was a wild land. A man had to watch it all the time.

Once he sat in a grove of cottonwoods, looking out, the sun glinting on a spidery trail of water; ahead of him too, a gnarled leaning trunk, a dying thing.

He took his knife from the back of his belt where it snugged next to his second gun, a snub-nosed, pretty, lightweight Smith and Wesson.

The knife wasn't as big or as heavy as a Bowie but shaped in a similar way: more weight at the end of the blade than at the other end. He spun the knife, gripping the blade between thumb and forefinger. Leaving his hand, it spun and sparkled in the dappled sunlight and embedded itself in the twisted tree with a satisfying *thunk*.

In his wild days he had been the best of the bunch as a knife-thrower, winning competitions with it. But he'd never used a knife on humans.

He hadn't lost his touch, though, that was for sure.

He dragged his mind from the past, back to the present. Such a short time since he had dragged back-shooting Daley Clegg back to the town called Reprobate in which Deputy Lem Gallaghan had made his home.

Nobody seemed to know who had given the town such a strange name. Some devilishly humorous cuss no doubt. A home for such a reprobate as Gallaghan. And another called Daley Clegg who had spat in the face of the town, killed one of its people.

But Clegg wasn't Gallaghan's business now. And he knew that the two men he sought, though completely merciless, were the kind that Daley Clegg had never been.

46

Two killers who traded under so many aliases that they had probably forgotten many of them themselves. Gallaghan hadn't been much help there. Too many of that stripe in the West, always had been, Gallaghan reflected: there but for the grace of the almighty . . . .

But a pattern had been set, and Gallaghan was trying to follow that pattern. Oh, Jehosophat, how much had he wanted to stay with Julie. But he owed her dead brother much more.

It had been a clean kill. No clues. The local law hadn't been able to tell the visiting deputy a thing. But had the two hired gunsters hit the wrong man? Seemed like it.

And now they were after the right one.

But now Gallaghan was figuring that he wasn't too far away from them. He had ridden the owlhoot trail. He had connections too.

Sheriff Trig Bestor had taken the handcuffs from the wrists of Daley Clegg and had tied his hands with rawhide in front of him so that he could guide his horse. The three men rode in single file with the older man and his deputy, Prince, flanking the prisoner, who seemed to be dozing in the hot sun when the sheriff started to cough again.

It was a bad one. It shook him like a storm. He swayed as if buffeted. Then he pitched from his horse like a high-falling log and his bulk hit the hard ground very forcibly.

47

Anxiously, Deputy Prince slid from his saddle, ran to his friend who lay motionless.

They hadn't tied Clegg's legs. He wasn't asleep either, had been waiting for something to happen. For a moment, the young deputy's back was turned towards him. Clegg left the saddle awkwardly, but both his feet hit the ground.

Prince heard him and began to turn, reaching for his gun. But Clegg's hands were already going up and over, roped, clenched like a club.

The knuckles caught the young man hard on the side of his face and he went sprawling. Clegg kicked him in the head and he lay still.

He was then almost side by side with his chief who lay as motionless as if he were dead.

Clegg found a jack-knife in the unconscious deputy's vest pocket. He managed to cut his bonds. Then he divested the two men of their armoury and placed it about his own person.

The sheriff was still alive but breathing very raggedly. Prince began to moan and stir. Clegg pointed the younker's own gun at him, but then he changed his mind, reversed the gun and slugged the younker with its barrel.

He took Prince's mount which seemed the best of the bunch. He let the two men lie, rode on. *Hard.* He began to figure that he should have killed them. But he didn't turn back. There was another scapegoat he aimed to send to Kingdom Come, at that!

\* \* \*

Armitage was the first to see the scarfaced man that night in the saloon. A card-school was under way and the man Armitage and Dougal had sought was involved.

Armitage also took a hand. Dougal stayed at the bar. They hadn't of course, acknowledged each other.

The place was not yet too crowded. A lot of the unhurried activity was, in fact, centred around the gaming-tables, particularly the largest, where Armitage had joined the scarfaced man and some of his friends, townies and visitors. A disgruntled player had dropped out and the chubby-faced Armitage had taken his place, was sitting directly across the table from the man whom he and his partner had sought.

Poker was the game and at the moment it looked as if Armitage was being fleeced, and by Scarface at that, who had a pile of chips in front of him.

Dougal wasn't sure whether his partner's ploy was the right one. He even wondered what Armitage had in mind. The demise of Scarface at the end of it all, of course; but when and how?

The area round the bar where Dougal stood was not too densely populated. Dougal had a good view of his partner and the other gamblers, the game that was the centre of attention of others as well as himself.

They had not talked for some time and, here in the bar-room, no signal had passed between them. When Armitage pulled the furious cat out of the bag it was almost as much of a surprise to Dougal as it was to others; no less than the other players at the table, whether they were friends of Scarface or not.

Armitage, leaning forward, shouted in tones of fury, 'You're cheatin' me, you bastard!'

And Scar, as furious himself it seemed, acted: it was like a scene from a fit-up playlet that the two antagonists had planned to stage. Half-rising, Scar reached down. But the muzzle of Armitage's Colt appeared over the edge of the table and the big blue-steel gun bucked and thundered. A yellow lance; a spurt of flame.

Scar staggered backwards, clutching at his throat from which blood jetted, vivid-red beneath the yellow light of the hanging lantern which bathed the table in its glow. Scar's chair went over behind him, and him with it, his hat paraboling and falling.

As if in a last clench of life, he still had a double-barrelled derringer in his fist which he must have pulled from beneath the table-top. He was pressing the trigger too, as his dying clasp let the gun go. It fell. But the heavy slug from the lethal weapon – always better at close range – and this was close! – was already speeding on its way.

It seemed to hit Armitage, and he staggered. But then he righted himself. And his gun was still in his hand.

'Let 'im by.' The voice came from the region of the bar.

Dougal had two guns out, his hands spread apart, the steel barrels winking, menacing the crowd. Half-crouching, Armitage moved to join his partner, his own gun still levelled.

They backed through a convenient side door and

50

hurried along an alley, Armitage moving in an ungainly manner.

'Always the grandstand,' Dougal said, thickly. Armitage, breathing hard, did not answer him.

Sheriff Bestor was back on his horse, lolling across its neck. 'I'll be all right now,' he said thickly. 'Get after that bastard.'

'Don't be stupid,' said Prince.

'Don't you talk to me like that, boy.'

'That bastard 'ull keep,' said the young deputy. 'We'll get 'im sooner or later. Right now I've got to get you back to town an' the doc. You can't ride any more, just follow me as close as you can.'

The elder man had nothing more to say, holding on grimly to his mount. Prince led the way, was mightily relieved when the town of Reprobate came in sight, with its lights and, in one spot, smoke and a few spurts of flame.

The fire at the jail was dampening down. But that place was no place to take a sick man. Followed by shouting questions which he didn't answer, the deputy backed his mount a little and led the other horse with its deadweight burden on to the doc's surgery.

# SEVEN

They got out of the settlement without having to shoot anybody else. It was a dark night, with only a pale sliver of moon peeping fitfully from behind lowering clouds.

They heard no sounds of pursuit. Folks had been taken by surprise. Maybe nobody had shot at one of bandit-leader Jonesy's boys before, let alone killed one stone dead. The killer and his partner hadn't seen anything of Jonesy that night; maybe in some way that was the reason for the delay in pursuit. *Jonesy!* A sardonic alias no doubt. Dougal and Armitage knew his stripe.

They rode hard, not actually speaking. But Armitage made painful grunting sounds from time to time and clung to his horse as if he loved the beast for all time.

Dawn was breaking when Armitage began to fall back behind his companion and Dougal reined in his mount, turned in the saddle.

'I'm hit,' said Armitage.

Dougal had figured that all along but hadn't

remarked upon it. He had figured that the slug from the scarfaced owlhooter's derringer had hit Armitage someplace, a flesh wound maybe – and he (Dougal) wasn't about to put his own neck in jeopardy for the sake of a partner's flea-bite.

But he turned his horse around and put him forward as he saw that Armitage was slowly slipping out of the saddle. He was in time to catch the man and lower him to the ground, dismounting slowly from his own mount as he did so.

Armitage had his scuffed leather vest fastened tightly across his chest, though the climate was warm, and would get warmer.

The garment stuck as Dougal began to open it and, as his saddle-pard pulled at the material the wounded man gave off an explosive sound of agony.

There was a bloody hole high up in Armitage's side. A slug from one of those nasty little sneak guns surely made a mess of human flesh if they hit at close quarters, Dougal reflected. This was no flea-bite.

Ahead of the two men, one supine, the other on one knee beside him, was a grove of tall, lank trees.

Armitage couldn't walk. The burly Dougal had to carry him, passing a stand of Spanish bayonet as he did so, and the sun becoming warmer on the back of his neck.

The two horses followed. Leaving his partner in the grass among the trees, Dougal went back to delve into his saddle-bags. Something caught his attention out of the corner of his eyes: a suggestion of movement.

He squinted against the sun.

There were riders approaching.

The doc put the sheriff to bed, where the big man went to sleep with astonishing rapidity. However, the little medico said his friend – and they'd known each other since they were kids – would be all right, that all he needed now was warmth and rest. He said that Trig had the constitution of a wagon-horse and maybe his night-ride had done him good, cleared his stupid head.

The doc was in fact more worried about the young deputy's head, which had had two nasty knocks this night. Prince sagged in a chair, obviously at the end of his tether now after his Herculean efforts in bringing his ailing chief back to the comfortable town of Reprobate which had been far less comfortable in recent times.

'I'm going to fix you up,' the little man said. 'And then you're going home to bed.'

'How about the jail?'

'It's being looked after, Everything will be looked after. The rowdy element are singing small now. There are plenty good folks here, me boy.'

'I know.'

Prince promised to go home and rejoin his widowed mother, another old friend of the little medico's.

The doc watched him go then went down to the jail-house to see if there were any more folk he could succour. Find some volunteers too, who would keep watch.

The fire was almost out. There were watchers, among them old Loney Dorman, who was anxious about the sheriff and his deputy; could he see them? Not yet, said the doc, maybe in the morning. Another old friend, Loney, a cannier man than most folks gave him credit for.

The jailhouse could be fixed. Already folks were planning to start work on it come morning, volunteers offering timber and tools.

Satisfied, the little doctor went back to his own bed. Reprobate was almost quiet again under pale moonlight and scudding clouds.

There was, though, an air of waiting.

Folks were up early in the morning. There was nothing ominous about that. There was a bustle. Sheriff Bestor was a lot better, brighter. There was yet no sign of Prince. But Loney turned up, and the doc allowed him to see the burly lawman, though with strict orders that the latter should remain in bed, wasn't well enough to get up yet.

What Loney told his lawman friend made Trig feel like getting up. But he was sensible enough to fight that urge. His journey last night had been a disaster and, although the doc had said Prince would be all right after a good rest, the chief worried about his deputy. Hell, that son-bitch, Daley Clegg, had a helluva lot to answer for!

Loney said he'd been thinking about Clegg, whom he'd had dealings with in the past. He had an idea where the back-shooting fugitive might be making for.

A settlement on the edge of the Sonora territory, a sort of open town which had never had a name as far as Loney knew, but which was virtually ruled by a mad Southerner called Jonesy, although he wasn't actually there himself much of the time.

'I'll take you there when you're fit.'

'All right,' Trig Bestor said.

The doc returned after visiting Prince, said the lad was healing fine but had been persuaded to stay in bed the rest of the day and the following night: his ma would see to that.

Things in the realms of lawdom were sort of in abeyance it seemed, no matter how many killers were on the run. But the rest of Reprobate was mighty busy, the sound of hammering resounding in the still air.

'I hope we don't get any rain,' the doc said.

But they did.

And it was widespread.


Lem Gallaghan had heard the thunder, had expected the rain. When it began he was in a spacious room in a way station with a meal in front of him which had been prepared by a brown-skinned girl with a beaming smile. She worked for the childless man and wife who ran the station, the corrals and barns and cabins which catered to stagecoaches and wayfarers.

Gallaghan wasn't the only person eating there, and the chow was mighty good. He had fried chicken and thinly sliced pork with beans done properly, not the canned variety which he'd often been glad of when on the trail; baked potatoes too, and something on the side; a kind of spicy relish, a border dish no doubt, maybe the cook's own recipe. There was an apple-and-currant-pie with custard, coffee you could stand a ladle in and some of the place's special whiskey, bourbon no less.

He sat back in his seat, replete, taking one of the couple of stogies that had been put beside his place. He lit up, blew smoke that wreathed his head.

The brown-skinned girl came back to clear the plates and he looked up at her and said, 'Mighty fine, honah. Mighty fine.'

Her pretty face dimpled, her dark eyes with a roguish twinkle. 'Thank you, suh,' she said.

Another time maybe, he thought. Another time.

But there was no time for dalliance now.

Even so, he could not yet force himself to rise.

This was a quiet time, a time for replenishment. He had to force himself to make the most of it. He had always been able to relax, stretching himself, and then loosening his muscles all over. He did that now. Blue smoke drifted above and he shut out the voices around him, which were not yet too obtrusive. People were leaving now . . . .

# EIGHT

'I'm gonna hang you,' the big leader said.

Jerking a thumb in the direction of his supine partner, Dougal said, 'You cain't hang him. He's half-dead already. Let 'im be.'

'I'm gonna take you both back and I'm gonna string you up for all to see. Nobody puts down one o' my boys an' lives to talk about it. I might hand you over to the women first. You'll like that, two fancy boys like yuhuns.'

'C'mon, Jonesy,' said Dougal. 'Have a sense of humour for Chrissakes.'

The big leader gave out with a booming laugh which his boys took up like a bunch of inebriated coyotes, while Jonesy spluttered, 'Get 'em up on their nags.'

This was done, Armitage having to be tied in the saddle, his arms around the cayuse's neck. The wounded professional killer was still breathing, but only just.

'Maybe I could work with them an' the whip,' said

Jonesy's *segundo*, who rode next to the big man. He was a stunted *mestizo* called Rigona who sported a black walrus moustache with spiked ends and always carried a stockwhip with a silver butt which he'd bought from a German feller in Sante Fe.

Rigona was Jonesy's enforcer and feared by many, particularly the women.

He didn't like women. Playthings! And the only person he looked up to in all the world was the big leader, who went along with him in his foibles, relished most of them. Now he said, 'Maybe. As long as you don't get too heavy-handed.'

'I could take their eyes off neat as slicing with a sabre,' Rigona chuckled, patting his blacksnake like it was a favourite dolly.

'I'm hungry,' said Jonesy. 'I know a place.'

'Maybe the one o' them two 'ull die,' said Rigona, petulantly.

'So he dies.' Those were the big leader's last words. He was uncertain-tempered and even his little dark sidekick couldn't push him too far.

Gallaghan looked up when the bunch entered the place. His eyes became startled, then hooded.

He knew the big leader by sight; and the little dark weasel who kept so close to him.

There was among the bunch a man with his hands tied behind his back.

Gallaghan recognized that man too, had had descriptions of him. He wondered what had happened to that man's partner, whatever that man called himself now, him and his partner. His partner who didn't seem to be around.

Dougal and Armitage. He had heard those names. He didn't know whether they were still using 'em or had picked others just as outlandish. Sort of mocking.

Smiling killers. Mocking everybody.

But this one wasn't mocking anybody now. And Gallaghan didn't know that this one's partner was outside tied to a horse, being watched by two more of the infamous Jonesy's boys. Armitage, whether dead or still alive.

Then Jonesy saw Gallaghan, spoke his name, was obviously surprised to see him there. But Jonesy was a smart one (maybe he'd even heard rumours and was playing his cards close to his chest) and he asked, 'You huntin' somebody, Lemuel boy?'

'Yes, old friend,' Gallaghan replied, stabbing a finger in the direction of the tall captive. 'That one.'

'I guess you came off second best then, *amigo*,' said the big man and at his side poisonous Rigona giggled like a spiteful cow-girl.

Daley Clegg was disgruntled.

Why hadn't he killed the sheriff and deputy when he had a chance?

Great snakes, they'd been on his heels for murder! And would be again. That cocky little son-bitch, Prince. And even old Trig, if he didn't die from his malady, and that hardly seemed likely.

And ahead of Daley was Lem Gallaghan. Another fancy lawman. God, Daley hated lawmen.

Maybe he'd catch up with Gallaghan. He'd take his spleen outa that big 'un's hide all right and leave his carcass for the buzzards.

But he couldn't keep riding for ever. He needed some things. He paused to figure out just where he was now; and he got that figured and got all cock-a-hoop again.

He made for the little homestead, and the sisters. He hoped they were still there. Hell, why wouldn't they be? He'd get what he wanted from them.

The youngest, Dru, was the prettiest. But the elder, Caroley, was the most inventive, and liked it kinda rough.

*Rough!* That was just the way Daley felt right now.

He saw the cluster of buildings in the distance, the wisp of smoke from a chimney. He spurred his horse. Then he slowed the beast again as he spotted something moving by the house.

He shaded his eyes with his hand. And he saw what he saw. A gig with a trotting horse, two people on the seat. He squinted.

A smallish figure, maybe a kid.

The other one wasn't big either. A woman maybe.

Daley's first inclination was to set his mount at a gallop towards them. But then he got some sense, some caution, and stayed put, watched the small equipage till it was out of sight, taking a different trail from the one he was following, though going backaways through the territory he'd already traversed.

He spurred his horse on. One of the girls came out as he reined in before the house. It was Dru, the pretty one, and she called him by name.

'You had visitors, huh?' he said. 'Who was that?'

'A neighbour visitin'.'

Caroley met him at the door and he was out of the saddle then and she flung her arms around him.

Hot thick coffee was soon forthcoming and the girls told him about the neighbour who lived about four miles away, they said.

Name of Julie, a widow, had a kid, a boy called Jonathon.

Daley had had a good meal and was in bed with Caroley – Dru's turn would come later, an' easing-off – when the man asked again about the neighbour lady and her son. And what he heard made his ears prick like a startled fawn's.

Julie's brother had recently been bushwhacked to death, a mystery, nobody caught. He had in the past been one of the wild boys who ranged the borderlands. His name had been linked with that of Lem Gallaghan – the girls knew Lem from the old days before he became a lawman. It was said he still visited Julie from time to time.

He had done so recently. He was after whoever had killed his friend.

'Do tell!' said Daley Clegg.

'C'mon, honey,' the girl said.

Daley grunted, moving. The nasty ankle he had

acquired while in the custody of Gallaghan was playing up again. But he wasn't going to let that faze him. Not yet anyway.

He was a mite breathless when he asked, 'What was that brother's name?'

'What brother?' Caroley gasped.

'That young widder-woman's brother, f' Pete's sake.'

'Chris Dakes.'

'Do tell,' exclaimed Daley for the second time.

He knew the name, had known its owner for a short time in the old days. He tucked the name and the knowledge away in the ragbag of his mind. But not too deep. The knowledge might come in handy, yes sir!

But there was the ankle. And other things first.

Sister Dru was tapping lightly but insistently on the bedroom door.

# NINE

The little dark girl came in from the back and her boss signalled to her to go away. But he was too late. The boys had spotted her and made sounds of appreciation.

'I told you there was a juicy filly here, didn't I?' said one of them to the friend at his side.

'Stay where you are, girl,' said Jonesy, his hand on the butt of his gun. He looked straight at the owner. 'Where's your wife, *amigo*? Call her out.'

She must have been close behind the girl but hidden by the curtain which separated the two rooms. She appeared. As raw-boned as her husband and, by her attitude, maybe even more fearless.

'What's your business?' she demanded.

'Just some sustenance, missus,' said Jonesy. 'We don't mean anybody any harm.'

But they had already done somebody harm, as was evidenced by the sight of the battered-looking Dougal. But then more evidence appeared as two more of the big leader's boys came in, carrying Dougal's partner, Armitage, slinging him down on the boards.

'He's cashed in, chief,' said one of them.

'You didn't have to bring him in here. Take him out again.'

They did this. Both the women had started forward, the younger expelling a little cry from her plump red lips.

'Everybody be still an' quiet,' Jonesy said.

Right then there was little else to do yet, or so it seemed.

But Lem Gallaghan spoke up, pointing a finger again at Dougal. 'I want him for murder.'

And nobody else with a gun out now, except Gallaghan himself, the muzzles of his Lightning Colt and his smaller back-up appearing over the table top.

He might have noticed that the little moustached *mestizo* – the one called Rigona – carried a whip like it was a talisman of some kind. But he could never have imagined – others hadn't before him – how fast the animal-like near-dwarf could be.

Not till the heavy thong slashed him across the forehead, taking his senses from him.

His Lightning went off, but the slug passed between the men in front of him and smashed a window-pane. Then both guns fell under the table and Gallaghan slumped across, face-down, blood already seeping from beneath his face.

They would have killed him. Rigona wanted to – a whip across his throat, the thong tightening. But, laughing, Jonesy said, 'Let 'im be. He's an old saddle-pard o' mine. He allus was a feisty 'un.'

Nobody could always understand the big man's moods, not even the equally moody and unpredictable Rigona. But he was the boss, the grand-stander, and they always did what he said. Men had died for arguing with him: he was *that* moody!

The whip had cut deeply into Gallaghan's forehead just below the hair line.

He was told that he'd been unconscious a long time.

When he came to he didn't know where he was, didn't remember what had happened. He only knew that his head felt like it was about to burst and that, below, it seemed a red-hot branding iron had been drawn across his skin, biting deeply into tortured flesh.

He was on something soft. Surely a bed. He flinched: somebody was bending over him.

A female voice said, 'Take it easy.'

He opened his eyes slowly and blinked at a middle-aged feminine face. Then, in a rush, he recognized it. And everything came to him and he asked, 'Why didn't they kill me?'

'The big fellow wouldn't let them, said you were an old friend o' his.' A male voice now, an accusing tone.

'He used to be. But that was a long time ago. I'm a deputy sheriff. I was after the man they'd got.'

'So you reckoned.'

'What did they do with him?'

'They took 'im with 'em. and the other one. The dead one.'

Stranger and stranger. But this was Jonesy after all!

'They took the girl with them,' said the woman, and there was an accusing note in *her* voice now.

The man said harshly, 'That little half-breed bastard wanted her, said she was Injun like him anyway.'

'We never had kids,' the woman said. 'An' she was like a daughter to us.'

Gallaghan felt himself sort of drifting away. He fought the thing, moved, raised his hand to his head and felt the bandage.

'That whip went in deep,' the man said. 'Like a knife. The little son-bitch wanted to cut you to ribbons, finish you, but the big feller wouldn't let 'im.'

'He made a mistake,' said Gallaghan, his senses back with him again. 'The big feller I mean. Jonesy.'

'I thought that was who he was,' the man said.

'I'll get the girl back for you.' Gallaghan pulled himself upright in the bed. 'Where're my togs?'

'You still got most of 'em on. And they left your guns on the floor.'

Gallaghan was on the edge of the bed. He hung his head. In there a hive of bees fought a civil war. He was leaning sideways like an aspen in the wind. He fought to straighten himself and sit on the edge of the bed. He made it, keeping his eyes closed then. Equilibrium, he thought, that's what I need.

'You aim to go then?' the man said.

Like hell, thought Gallaghan. But he said, 'I do,' and told himself he meant it.

'I'm coming with you,' the man said.

'Both of us are comin' with you,' the woman said.

Gallaghan thought, I should've started blasting as soon as I had the guns out. There was only four of 'em counting Jonesy. Two of them at the back, the rest outside, maybe only the two of them he'd seen with the body. Would the little whip-artiste have been too fast for him even then, him with the edge, two guns over the table? Maybe. The thought galled him.

Now what were these two burbling about? He looked from one to the other of them, thankful that he could get his eyes open without his head falling off.

Two gauntish faces full of determination.

'I can shoot,' said the man. 'I've been around. I can shoot well.'

'So can I,' said the woman.

He felt too hurt and worn to argue with them. Bestir yourself, bucko, he thought, work it out.


The boy was named Jonathon and he was ten years old. He was chopping wood in the cool of the going-down sun when he saw the rider coming across the plains.

This was the back of the house and the outlook was flat till the horizon was broken by a stand of cotton-woods in the distance, the sun behind them still with some power in it before twilight came. Jonathon had to shade his eyes with his hand.

The front of the house looked out towards the small town of Baker's Dip. Jonathon's uncle, Christopher, used to call the place Dake's Dip because that was his surname, as it was the surname of his sister, Julie, of course, before she got married.

But Christopher was gone, bushwhacked not so long ago. Jonathon's Dad was gone too, killed by a wild horse. So there was just Jonathon and his mom left now, except for the elderly Mexican, José, who helped from time to time. But he was in town now, getting some supplies.

The place had a few horses, a few cattle, a vegetable- and flower-garden. They'd make it. But this was a melancholy time.

Seeing the horseman clearer now, Jonathon did not recognize him. The man raised his hand above his head in the time-honoured peace sign. And, if hesitantly, Jonathon did the same.

At first he thought that the rider might be Lem Gallaghan returning. But he had realized that it was maybe too soon for that. He knew that his mom feared for Lem and what Lem was out to do, to avenge his old friend, her brother Christopher.

Jonathon realized that the approaching stranger was not as big as Lem, did not ride the way Lem did, did not have the horse called Rip.

Looked harmless enough, though.

Ugly. But grinning like Jonathon and he were old friends from way back.

Maybe he was an old friend of Jonathon's mom's. A memory tugged at the back of the boy's mind but did not stay.

Julie had obviously heard the hoofbeats. She came out through the back door.

Jonathon turned his head, asked, 'You know him, Mom?'

'Maybe. I'm not sure.'

# TEN

They were the Picketts, Anna and Herb. Both pretty
taciturn, riding into the sunset with Lem Gallaghan. He
had learned things about them, but it had been sort of
a bit like pulling teeth. Bit surprising, though, as well.

Herb had said his missus could shoot well. Gallaghan
could believe that – after he learned that she'd been a
trick shooter in a circus.

He didn't ask her if she'd ever shot at any people.

He figured that, married to a woman like that, Herb
should be a more than decent shooter himself. Any
man in the same position – particularly here in the
lawless West where guns were paramount – wouldn't
want to be completely outdone by some filly.

Anna was no filly. No beauty either.

All in all, though, Gallaghan decided he liked these
two taciturn folk. Hell, he was no chatterbox himself,
an' that was a fact.

Herb wasn't sure where Jonesy's hideout was, but he
figured they could find out. And Gallaghan was

reminded of Jonesy again. And he realized he had made a hell of a mistake. Maybe he'd deserved to be whipped.

He should have told the big leader that he, Gallaghan, as a deputy sheriff, was after professional killer Dougal for the murder of an old friend, Christopher Dakes. Jonesy would have listened, come through maybe. For, once upon a time, Jonesy, Christopher and Gallaghan had ridden together, a trio.

The old days. They were coming back to him now.

After the Civil War. Three youngsters, little more than wet-nosed sprigs who had fought for the South. Broke, hungry, tired, they had ridden into a tent-and-clapboard town which seemed to have grown up suddenly out of no-place, only to discover that it was a haunt of folks of all stripes, most of them the hated so-called 'carpet-baggers' who, with their cheap goods (and expensive foodstuffs) were covering the impoverished areas of the South-west like lice.

The three boys had been refused food that they couldn't pay for: nobody had offered them even scraps that they might've given to a starving cur-dog.

They had been caught stealing and had had to fight their way out. Gallaghan had been on the hard-packed mud of a tent-floor, a big man with a knife, a knee in his belly, the blade aimed at his throat.

Christopher had flung himself forward and grappled with the man, had had inflicted on him the facial scar he'd carried for the rest of his life. Until a bush-whacker's bullet had finished that life for him. They had shot their way out. Jonesy had killed a man, earned a price on his big, reckless head.

The three had split up, but Christopher, quite by accident, had met up again with the big Southerner and thus had earned a price on his own head, which had finally been quashed by the efforts of Sheriff Trig Bestor, whose friend Lem Gallaghan was on the straight and narrow now, a law deputy no less.

Gallaghan did not tell his new saddle-partners about all this. He wasn't the sort to look ahead too far and worry about it. He figured that things would work out for themselves eventually – with a bit o' pushing that was. And maybe he'd even live to tell another tale.

He hoped his two new friends weren't riding into something they couldn't handle.

But he didn't worry about that either.


Daley didn't think the woman had been at all co-operative. She hadn't answered any of his questions properly. She had given him coffee and hot cakes, but she was now looking at him as if he was a coyote caught in her hen-coop.

She was a beauty, tough, there was no denying that. He figured she owed him. She owed him *something*.

They were in the kitchen, facing each other across the scrubbed, gleaming-white table. He got up from his chair and went round the table.

She had his stripe now. His attentions were obvious.

There was still the sound of Jonathon chopping

wood outside. She had told him to finish his chores while she and the visitor talked.

She swung her chair around. Eel-like, she eluded the man's grasp. She turned, moved fast, started to get the drawer open at the right-hand side of the Dutch dresser.

He was quicker than she expected. He moved like a predatory animal. He grabbed her by the shoulders, swung her around, banged her back against the dresser. Crockery fell with a crash.

He had Julie bent backward and was thrusting at her, his face at hers, when Jonathon came through the back door with a formidable-looking log in his fist.

He struck Daley hard on the back of the head.

Daley went down in a tangle.

The boy bent over him, wide-eyed, the improvised weapon still poised in his hand.

'Is he dead, Mom?'

'No, just stunned. Go get some rope from the barn. Hurry!'

Jonathon dropped his log and scuttled away. Julie skirted the man's prone form. She got the old Dragoon Colt out of the drawer. The long-barrelled weapon hung heavily in her hand. She pointed it down at the unconscious man and said, 'I oughta kill you.'

'I tell yuh,' said Dru, 'he sorta went back the way he came. Well, not exactly that maybe, but still as if he was sorta back-trackin'. That way.' She pointed. 'Almost the way Julie went back.'

Caroley looked at her sister, pursed her lips. Then

she said, 'Come to think of it, he asked about Julie. He saw her leaving before he got here. Seems he knew Julie's brother, Christopher, the one who was so mysteriously killed. He knows Lem Gallaghan too.'

'I remember Lem Gallaghan,' said Dru. She giggled. 'I'm sure you remember 'im well – you wuz kinda sweet on him. A big man for a big girl, you said.'

'Hell, Dru-baby, that was a long time ago. He's a high muckamuch lawman now, ain't he? He wouldn't give the likes of you an' me a second glance.'

'I dunno.' Dru scratched her head. 'I sort of gathered that Daley Clegg hates Gallaghan anyway. And Gallaghan was a friend of Christopher Dakes, is a friend of Julie's also. I allus wondered whether there'd been somep'n between 'em some time or another.'

'Wait a minute! Do you think Daley is aiming to call on Julie?'

'I think it's time we paid Julie a return visit, sister.'

It was dark when they got to Julie's place and dismounted, went through the back door which was unlocked. They heard muffled noises but couldn't see anything. Caroley knew where the lamp was: she scratched a lucifer, lit it. Daley was on the floor bound and gagged, had been trying to shout, and chomp at the cloth that had been stuffed in his mouth.

The two girls were good horsewomen. They always carried weapons.

Dru brought forth her knife and cut Daley free.

The man spluttered, 'They've gone for the law – we gotta get outa here'

'You had to try it, didn't you?' Caroley said. 'But you bit off more than you could chew.' She was grinning; Daley was still spitting.

His horse was still outside. The girls accompanied him. They took a devious trail.

'They took my weapons,' the man said. 'I've got to get some weapons.' He was slowing down.

Caroley said, 'You don't get no weapons from us, bucko. We got you free, figured we owed you that I guess.'

'I know the woman is a friend o' yorn.' The man was almost whining now. 'I just wanted her to tell me where Lem Gallaghan had gone.'

'Gallaghan wouldn't have told her,' Dru said.

'On your way,' said Caroley, and she had her rifle with the muzzle tilted in Clegg's direction. 'We're finished with you. If I see your ugly face near our place I'll shoot. On sight, I promise you.'

'She said it.' Dru sounded just as adamant. 'Get moving – before we change our minds an' drop you here an' now.'

Daley Clegg's rejoinder was colourful and obscene. But he had his spurs to his horse, which bounded forward, and the breeze took most of the words away.

Sheriff Trig Bestor and his deputy, young Prince, were riding again. The latter had a bandage on his head, a reminder of the set-to he'd had with the fugitive Daley Clegg. It wasn't a bulky bandage. Prince could get his hat on, tilted at a rakish angle. The doc had said the laddie hadn't gotten concussion or anything like that.

The sheriff was spry again, had now gotten completely over his dose of croup. Anyway, they sort of had a minder now, both of 'em. Old Loney Dorman, lisping like an excited baby (the others had never heard him so talkative before), who figured he knew where the murderous fugitive might be making for. Loney, more astute than any of his fellow townies had ever figured, was riding high, wide 'n' han'some again, he said: it was like old times.

First off they reached Julie's little ranch. Loney and Prince had never met the girl and her boy before, but the sheriff was an old friend.

They hit a surprise. Clegg had been here, had been captured by Julie and young Jonathon, trussed while she went for help. Clegg had been let loose, his bonds cut, his horse gone. If Julie had suspicions about who had let the man loose, she didn't voice them. A town posse had gone after Clegg. Trig Bestor didn't seem to set much store by the local law but didn't actually say so.

He had an idea of who the culprits were who'd set Clegg free. But he didn't voice his suspicions about that either.

'Will you be all right?' he asked.

'We'll be all right, Trig,' said Julie.

'Sure thing,' said Jonathon. He was at the kitchen window. He added, 'Riders comin'.'

The sheriff joined him. 'It's Fat Capes an' his boys. They don't seem to have any prisoner.'

They hadn't. The obese man toting a badge said they

hadn't seen a soul, the fugitive had had too good a start. To go further would be outside his jurisdiction he said.

'It's outa mine,' said Trig Bestor. 'But we want that boy. We want 'im bad. Did you call on the two sister-girls?'

'No-oo. Like I said—'

Trig cut in. 'We'll take over.'

They called on the girls. Caroley, defiant, said Daley was an old friend of theirs, they'd had to give him some sort of chance.

Dru, placatingly, said, 'He ain't got any weapons or any tucker. He ain't got nothin'. We'll ride a ways with you, show you the trail he took.'

'You wuz allus jealous 'cos he thought more o' me than he did o' you,' Caroley said.

'Horse-shit,' said Dru, and she led the way, the boys following her. Her sister, swearing under her breath, brought up the rear.

Anna, it seemed, was good all round with her hands. Gallaghan could just imagine her spinning a revolver over and over in her long fingers in her sharpshooting days. She had fixed a sort of long plaster on his fore-head.

He had a headache. But the whiplash groove did not burn like before and now they were riding across level land with soft grass under the horses' hooves and there was no jolting.

Night had fallen but there was a pale, almost ghostly moon.

They could see quite a lot of the terrain in front of them and around. There was not much vegetation. Not until they saw the skeleton-like tree, all alone in the wide expanse, with the ghostlike thing dangling from one of its outstretched branches.

It was the corpse of the professional killer who had called himself Armitage. Jonesy had promised to hang him and had done just that, hadn't waited till they got to the hideout. But there was no sign of Armitage's partner, Dougal.

Jonesy had left all of Gallaghan's gear with him, hadn't even taken his knife as a souvenir. Gallaghan took the knife from the back of his belt and he cut Armitage down.

Anna said that, of course, the man had been dead long before he was strung up. Herb said maybe the corpse had been left as a sort of warning. He said that that was some knife that Gallaghan had, though it wasn't a Bowie. Hell, it was fancier than a Bowie.

Anna looked from one to the other of the two men in a sort of amazement. She insisted that they bury the corpse. They had no shovel. Herb had a knife. It wasn't as good as Gallaghan's, but it would serve. They made a shallow grave and put Armitage in it and covered him up.

Gallaghan had more reflecting to do. Jonesy – he had always been Jonesy even in the old days – had always had a wickedly sardonic sense of humour. The big laughing cuss with the Deep South voice and the twinkling blue eyes. He had chosen his ways. Ways that were different from those of his two old saddle-mates, Gallaghan and Dakes, the latter turned good but already gone, lost. Have I turned good, Gallaghan reflected?

Jonesy had always been unpredictable. Moody.

The other side of the fence: that's where Jonesy was now – and his old friend, Gallaghan, was toting a badge.

And there was still Dougal.

They rode on. Herb, Anna – and Lem. Who thought, to Hades and back if that had to be: there was no turning back now.

He wished his two new friends would turn back. But he knew they wouldn't. A girl they loved was in peril. And Gallaghan wasn't alone any more.

# ELEVEN

The two girls reined in, and the three men also, and Dru said, 'This is where we parted company with Daley.' She pointed. 'He went over that small hill. There's a trail up an' over.'

'I know it,' said Loney.

Sheriff Bestor asked a question. 'Have you seen Lem Gallaghan? You know him, don't you?'

'We know him, yeh. But we ain't seen 'im in a coon's age.'

'That's right,' said Caroley. She sniggered. 'Dru 'ud remember if we had see'd Lem all right wouldn't you, Dru honey?'

'Horse-shit,' said Dru, her favourite expletive it seemed.

'I ought to charge you two with helpin' a fugitive to escape,' said the sheriff. 'But right now I just ain't got the time. You take it easy, y'hear?'

'We will.' It was like a mocking duet.

But as the three horsemen reached the top of the rise before going down the other side, they looked back, and the girls, still sitting their horses, waved their hands gaily.

'Goddam strumpets,' said old Loney, cackling. Then the sight of the girls was gone and the men were on their way again, the old one in the lead like a bird-dog.

A long way from their home town they found other places, most of which Loney knew from the old days. They hadn't changed all that much, he said. This was the polyglot melting-pot of the lawless borderlands.

A gambling town called Ace Hole was run by a king-pin called Long Perce, an old friend of Loney's whom the trio met up with in The Wideawake Saloon.

Questioned, Perce told them a story about a fast-shooting gambling man who wasn't quite fast enough with his iron one night and was shot to death, straight-forward, outside a privy. And Perce, who didn't miss much, remembered the two quiet strangers – bounty men or something like that, he'd figured – who disappeared after the killing.

The executed man's rich poke wasn't even taken. Professionals doing a job, Perce figured – to hell with 'em, he had a business to run.

He remembered, though, that the two jaspers had stayed overnight with the Widow Small down the street a piece.

The trio visited the hatchet-faced woman who couldn't tell them much. Nice young men, she said, bridling like an old mare fighting a new bit. They'd been asking about a friend of theirs, she said, a drummer she thought, who had left just before they arrived.

82

'Wonder who that was,' said Sheriff Bestor as they rode on.

Seemed like they were going in the right direction, for, at the last moment, the widow had remembered another caller who'd visited, asking about the two nice young men. Her description fitted Len Gallaghan. Nobody it seemed had seen anybody resembling Daley Clegg; not even Long Perce, who'd known Daley.

'He couldn't be in everyplace all the time,' Loney said, a superfluous remark if ever there was one. The other two had never known the lisping oldster to talk so much.

Anyway, Loney still figured that Clegg was making for the hideout that had been mentioned before. Back of a settlement behind the hills on the edge of the Sonora territory, he said.

He remembered a stopping-place on the way to there, a stores and eating-place run by a couple, Anna and Herb Pickett.

But, when they got there, the place was locked up, quiet.

'Wonder what happened to those two?' the old man said. 'They were roamers who had settled, never moved very far then as I remember.'

The three had dismounted. They skirted the building, young Prince with his hand on the butt of his gun. There were an outhouse, a couple of privies, not much cover otherwise, no trees or rock outcrops, no stands of brush, mesquite or cacti. The surroundings were well kept, well swept.

Then Trig Bestor gave a small exclamation and the other two joined him at the front of the building. He had found blood on the soil.

'I'm gonna try an' get in there,' he said.

'Yeh, I'd like to know . . .' Loney's voice tailed off. He took out his jack-knife.

It didn't take him long to get the front door open.

They discovered that the interior was as spick and span as the outside. But there were smears of blood near the door as if a body had been dragged in – or dragged out. Or both ways.

The upstairs was warm and clean, the beds made, no more mysterious signs.

Outside again, Loney fastened the door up again as best he could. He walked, leading his horse, looking for sign, found nothing.

'Maybe we'll find somep'n as we go on,' he said. 'We'll make for the settlement I told you about, huh?'

'Sure,' said Trig.

'I guess it'll be dark afore we get there,' Loney said. On his horse again, he fell in with his two partners.

Later, however, they picked up tracks of horses, quite a bunch.

Loney said, 'Fancy bastards! They must've covered their tracks backaways. Like goddam Injuns.'

'Mebbe there's an Injun with 'em,' said Prince.

Unspeaking now, Loney dismounted. He had no trouble following the tracks then. There was still light, the sun low but bright.

The old man chuckled. 'I don't want to get us all-fired lost. That settlement is well hidden and can be approached in more than one way. An' then some! By a devious trail if you don't want to get spotted too soon. The kind of devious trail that Jonesy and his bunch would use in case there were lawmen waitin' for 'em.'

'You think this bunch we're following is Jonesy's?'

'Could be. But he might be goin' home now. A devious man used to devious trails, that's Jonesy.'

'Hell, you've lost me already,' said young Prince.

'We'll do what you say anyway, old friend,' said Trig. 'Rest our butts. Give ourselves an' the horses some sustenance.'

They had got some extra supplies from Widow Small back in Ace Hole. She had finally mellowed, doubtless thinking of Prince as a nice young man like the two partners the trio had been asking about; one of 'em already in his grave, as Sheriff Trig Bestor later affirmed, wondering, though, what had happened to his main deputy, Lem Gallaghan.

The sun was down but the night was not as cold as it could get sometimes, an irritating phenomenon. They did not light a fire, drank cold, bottle-coffee laced with rum, ate pork-and-stuffing sandwiches, canned beans. They smoked, praising the widder-woman after all. The horses cropped, then slept with wet noses. The men got into their blankets and snoozed also, their guns not far from their paws.

It was a misty morning and they set out before the sun began to rise. They found the other trail that Loney had mentioned and they hit the hills, the smallish bluffs rising to the right of them rather than the left, as the old man had first had it figured, admitted now that he must have been wrong.

'Long time since I was around here before.'

But later he added, 'I'm right, I'm sure I'm right.' And his two partners, neither of whom (not even Trig) knew this trail at all, had to go along with that.

Then Loney added that he figured there were two lots of folk that had travelled this trail, the bigger bunch first, then a smaller one, maybe only three or four folk. He wondered whether the second riders might have something to do with his old friends, Anna and Herb Pickett.

'Why would a woman go with her husband to follow a bunch of owl-hunters?' Trig Bestor wanted to know.

'Not an ordinary woman,' said Loney enigmatically. 'A woman who can shoot better an' straighter than you an' me.' Then he was off the saddle, peering at the ground. 'Sort of a short cut here someplace I think,' he pronounced.

# Part 2

# WILD JUSTICE

# TWELVE

His name was Bertram Jewell. He was a stocky man with a small paunch who looked somewhat older than he was, didn't mind, figured that might be to his advantage. He kept his square, pink face unmoustached with a genial, open look. He figured that was definitely to his advantage.

He always wore dark broadcloth and a string tie. He had a smooth Easternized accent that impressed folk. He had been a Pinkerton operative until he was found to be blackmailing clients, had been lucky not to go to jail. He had started up on his own, calling himself a range detective.

He still had blackmail on his mind, though, figured it was easy if you picked the right marks, made sure they were rich first of all of course.

He had something in mind.

He decided that it was time he visited that fat, oily go-between, broker-cum-set-up-man, Brackley.

He went quietly on horseback by devious trails. Not

89

the train; nor the gig and two horses he might have hired if he wanted to look mightily important.

Brackley was surprised to see him, probably hadn't expected to ever see him again, asked formally but rather nastily as was his way, 'What do you want, Mr Jewell?'

'Just some information. Mr Brackley. Just a little important information.

'I sell information sometimes. I never give it away.'

Without being asked Jewell had seated himself in the less comfortable chair on the opposite side of the desk from the fat man ensconced in his comfortable armchair with cushions.

Jewell toted a double-barrelled derringer in a specially made shoulder-holster, though this was actually nearer to his armpit, fastened snugly with straps.

He had perfected his draw and could shoot straight. He was quite fast. He had disarmed men, pointing at them the deadly little weapon which, at close range, could blow a huge hole in human flesh. But he had never killed anybody.

He knew that Brackley kept a pistol in the drawer in front of his fat belly.

What he didn't know right now was that Brackley's sneak weapon had been taken from him by a certain forthright individual, a tall lawman called Lem Gallaghan.

From this the fat man had learned a little lesson. Accordingly he had had a spring device fitted by a local craftsman, this being under the overhang of the desk and within easier reach of his hand than the drawer sneak-out had been; the pistol, a Remington with a cut-down barrel, held snugly, but springing out at a grip of agile fingers – and the fat man could be fast when he wanted to be.

He said to Jewell, 'I was going to put some more business your way. But I didn't know where you were, thought maybe you'd got something else going for you.'

'Oh, yes,' said Jewell, obviously unimpressed. They were like two poker-players with a pile of chips between them, neither of them aiming to give an inch.

But suddenly Jewell became impatient, made a show of it. 'I want to know who was the hirer for the last job, the top man, the money-man.'

'I don't know who he is. He used a go-between as well.'

'You'd find out. You've got connections all over, I know that. You'd make it your business to find out, you and the rest of your breed. You're like a damn' fat spider, catching things. You certainly caught me.'

'And paid you well.'

'Not enough. And I know ways of making more. I'd even cut you in if you co-operate.'

'Don't try your tricks on me, boy. You haven't got the right cards.' As if they were indeed playing cards and Jewell hadn't got a good hand after all.

Maybe it was the 'boy' that did it. Jewell had always thought of himself as a mature man, and a very smart one. He reached for his derringer and he got it out, sleek as if bathed in oil.

'That'll get you no-place.' This wasn't one of those young, professional killers. It wasn't Lem Gallaghan. None of that stripe, lawful or lawless. This was just a smooth-talking confidence man who, it seemed, was trying to use new tactics which, Brackley figured, didn't suit him at all.

'You tell me what I want to know or I'll shoot you,' said Jewell.

But he sounded kind of uncertain now. The fat man wasn't quaking in his blubber like Jewell had expected him to do.

But he had to play his hand out now to the end. 'Take that little sneak-gun out of the drawer carefully and put it on the desk.'

'What gun?' It was like a game all right.

'Don't mess with me. Do like I told you.'

'All right.'

Brackley reached to the drawer, reached lower. Jewell watched him in a hypnotized sort of way, not realizing that the wicked twin muzzles of his own little gun had dropped, the weapon sloping in his fist towards the top of the desk rather than at the person it was supposed to menace.

Brackley, the small Remington springing into his hand (he had practised too!), fired across the desk, the muzzle of the weapon tilted slightly upwards.

The butt of the gun was warm in his fist. It bucked satisfyingly. The bullet struck the other man in the middle of his temple and pushed him forclbly back in the chair, so that it tilted. The derringer left the man's hand, made a little curve, hit the desk and nestled among some papers.

The chair went over backwards, Jewell with it. He hit the floor with the back of his head. His head rolled sideways and blood smeared the carpet, smeared the staring eyes.

The chair righted itself, finally stopped rocking. There was a stillness, a quiet, the end of a short spasm of violence – and even the blue smoke was dispelling itself against the ceiling and the smell of cordite was dissipating.

Brackley put the Remington pistol down on the desk. It was a pretty gun which didn't look at all harmful now. Brackley stared. He could only see the bloodied side of Jewell's head, none of the face at all. This view of the body was hidden by the desk. Brackley did not rise, did not seem to be able to do anything yet. He didn't know whether the man who now lay dead on the carpet had ever killed anybody. He, Brackley, certainly hadn't, though he had done many other things to the human spirit of many folks who had passed his way.

He was startled into some sort of awakening by his office door being flung open. Through it came the old caretaker who, in fact, had let Jewell into the building. The limping old-timer had a sawn-off shotgun in his fists.

The fat man rose, his eyes wild. He babbled, 'Jube, he tried to kill me. I didn't mean to do him so bad.'

# THIRTEEN

Anna, Herb and their new friend, Lem, hit the settlement that Herb remembered. They had ridden all night under the light of a pale moon and they now knew they had to rest.

But not right yet.

This was a lawless town full of every kind of folk of all nationalities and customs and various stages of venality. Most of them were still talking about the explosive happenings that had taken place here very recently.

Not particularly unique maybe. But mightily interesting.

Anna and Herb knew folk here who had called in at their place while travelling.

The bleary-eyed, early-morning visitors were told of how a young hardcase had savagely killed one of big Jonesy's boys (the one with the scar), had been shot and wounded himself but had escaped with the help of his partner but with Jonesy and his boys in full cry after them.

Herb was able to tell his tale in turn. Of how Jonesy and his boys had caught up with the fugitives and that one of them was already dead, the other one being taken to Jonesy's hideout.

Herb wanted to know whether Jonesy and his boys had passed this way again, was told they hadn't. That figured!

Jonesy had the Picketts' girl. The listeners remembered that fine, dark girl. Dwarfish Rigo had fancied her. That nasty little bastard, even the most venal among them couldn't stand him!

Herb Pickett said to Lem Gallaghan, 'The gang must've chased the two boys our way, sort of back tracking, then, going back to the hideout they would'n'nve taken the other trail, missing this place. There are two trails to the hideout y'see, looped kinda, then coming back into each other. Both of 'em very rough. Jonesy's got a bolthole with two ways out. That's why the law have never gotten 'is ass.'

Herb turned to his wife. 'I want you to stay here, honah.'

'Fat chance,' she snorted. 'You'll need me.'

'Let's get some rest anyway,' said Gallaghan, placatingly.

They'd had grub, coffee, a tot each of smething stronger. Anna joined an old Mexican lady she'd known from way back. She'd be given a good bed after washing-up. Herb and Lem went to the bath-house and from there to a battered but clean estabishment which called itself a hotel. But they did so well they overslept and it was Anna who had to awaken them. And she had some mighty interesting news to impart.

Three more arrivals had hit the settlement.

Sheriff Trig Bestor, Deputy Prince, and old Loney Dorman.

Loney said to the Picketts, 'We stopped at your place. We wondered what had happened.'

They told the three new arrivals what had happened. With Gallaghan putting in his two cents' worth from time to time.

Eventually Daley Clegg's name cropped up. Nobody had seen him. Loney said, 'I figure he's making for the hideout.' He chuckled. 'Like everybody else seems to be. Sooner or later, as they say. Daley picked a tortuous route.'

Anna Pickett, who hadn't said much so far, suddenly chimed in. 'Daley's here in this place. I've seen him.'

They all looked at her as if they thought she'd gone suddenly loco. And her husband said, 'I didn't know you ever knew Clegg.'

'Are you sure it was him?' Sheriff Bestor asked.

'I'm sure. Although I only caught a glance of him on the street before he disappeared.'

'He's a disappearing kind of gent all right,' said Loney. 'I was beginnin' to think the earth had swallowed him.'

'I knew him as a kid,' Anna said. 'He was brought up in our neighbourhood. And he was a hardnosed little scut even then. I think I know where he might be now.'

They all looked at her, open-mouthed.

'Wherezat?' said Loney.

'He has a cousin. They were very close. You might remember her, Herb. She came to our place a couple of times with a travellin' fit-up group. Some o' the girls I used to know. Run by a skelington-man – that's what you called him – named Burlington. That's what he called himself anyway.'

'Yeh, I remember 'im.'

'There was a little redhead called Lucy. She's the cousin of Daley Clegg. She found other work. She's here. She's a fancy whore. If Clegg's hiding out, waiting, I reckon that's where he'll be. I don't reckon any other folk will know of their relationship. They'd probably think he's just another customer.'

'Ye-eh,' said Herb weakly.

His wife turned on Gallaghan and asked. 'How's your head, big feller?'

'Fine, ma'am.'

A remarkable female. Not only a trick-shooter (he believed all of that now) but a fine nurse as well. She had put a sort of plaster across his brow and now his hat fitted him right good. If he had a slight headache that was probably because of the oversleeping, which he was ashamed of now.

'You know that place, Anna?' asked Trig Bestor, an old friend renewing an acquaintanceship long broken.

'I think I can find it,' was the quick reply.

'This is my move,' said Gallaghan just as quickly. 'An' surely one man is less likely to be spotted. I can handle it.'

Nobody disputed this. Clegg was only one man after all.

'You take care of Anna, Lem, y'hear,' said Herb.

'Of course, *amigo*. She'll come right back.'

'C'mon then,' said the redoubtable lady.

Loaded for bear, thought Gallaghan. He certainly was! Jonesy, with his strange moods, strange impulses, strange loyalties had left his old saddle-partner everything. Two prime shooters with revolving death-holes, and plenty of cartridges; Winchester repeating rifle; a fine knife – and even the little sneak-pistol that Gallaghan had taken from that fat toad, Brackley, the last time he'd visited the scheming hypocrite.

'Lead the way,' he said. 'But keep in cover.'

'I can't see how I can do both,' Anna said caustically. 'But I'll try.'

Lucy had been out shopping. She had locked the room-door after her. When she returned, unlocked it, opened it, Daley came awake, reaching for his gun on the bedside table.

He'd been stretched out on the bed with his boots off.

'It's only me,' Lucy said.

He let the gun go, asked, 'See anything?'

'We-ell, no. But I met one o' the other girls an' she told me there're some new folks just arrived, looks like a posse of some sort. And with them are the Pickett couple who run the way stores, y'know?'

'Why would they leave that?' Daley asked, bleary-eyed, peevish.

'I wouldn't know, would I?'

Daley scowled, wordless now, began to put himself to rights.


I shouldn't have let that woman come, Gallaghan thought. That grand woman. I let my passion get the better of my discretion.

It brings an uncertainty, he thought.

He would have felt even more uncertain had he known what was going on behind him.

Herb Pickett looked at Sheriff Bestor, said, 'I've got to go, Trig. She ain't even got her gun. It's in a special sheath she made herself and fixed under the cantle on her saddle. It's a fine gun, chased in silver and with an ivory butt. A specially-made Peacemaker. I've got the rifle.' He sloped it.

'Go on, Herb,' Bestor said. 'But keep outa sight an' watch yourself.'

'I will. I'll use the side door.'

They were in an old *rathskellar*. The sheriiff knew the owner.

They watched Herb go. He disappeared. They waited. But for what?

# FOURTEEN

At about the same time that Herb left the *rathskellar*, Daley Clegg was leaving through the back door of the so-called hotel where redhead Lucy had her crib. Back-door exits were the norm here. Had Daley been spotted – which he wasn't – nobody would've cared a hoot.

He went along the backs of town, past the privies and the out-houses and the pig-pens. This settlement was in no way being a cowtown: beef was for suckers, unless you stole it and sold it on, or made a prime meal of it.

Daley wasn't quite sure what he meant to do. He'd bet a couple of dollars to a plug of chawin' baccy that Gallaghan had fixed up with that bunch and was with them right now. And he wanted Gallaghan, wanted him so bad that it was an ache in his gut.

But, then again, he mustn't go half-cocked. Maybe it would be better to make for the hideout right off. Jonesy would take him in. He could be a help to Jonesy, had been before. He could wait till things cooled down and then he could get after Gallaghan when neither that son-bitch or anybody else expected it.

He reached an alley that he knew well, had already used earlier that morning. It led to a curve of the higgledy-piggledy main street, if you could call it a main street at all.

He paused, and then he spotted the other person at the other end of the alley. A woman, half-turned away from him, seemingly looking up the street. But as if she wanted to be unnoticed as well.

It was as if she felt his eyes on her, though it had only been a bit of a glance he'd given her so far, hesitatingly. But then she turned round towards him and he saw her face and recognized her.

The Pickett woman from the way station. He hadn't on his recent meandering trail come in sight of that place, hadn't wanted to.

What was she doing here?

He hoped she hadn't, in turn, recognized him.

He hastened forward, looking ahead. Then he spotted the man coming towards him along the backs of town and he could hardly believe his eyes.

It was that bitch's husband and he was carrying a rifle, which he lifted when he saw Daley Clegg.

Daley drew; fired. He was very fast.

Herb hadn't gotten his rifle high enough, levelled. The spinning slug from Daley's Colt bored through his shoulder and spun him around, the rifle falling from his grasp.

He fell on his back.

Daley heard thudding footsteps in the alley behind him. The woman wore riding boots.

Still holding his gun, Daley skirted the man on the littered ground and ran. He didn't want a shoot-out that might bring the settlement down round his ears.

The livery stables was just round a corner up ahead. His horse was half-ready.

He reached the place, shouldered aside the hostler's wide-eyed kid, grabbed his saddle from the hook that had supported it. He had left many towns swiftly like this. And made it.

He made it now. Hitting the high plains without yet any sounds of pursuit behind him. And, ahead, the hills beckoned him.

Anna was the first to reach her husband, who was trying to sit up, his shirt sodden red at the shoulder. An oldster came along, then a younger man, buttoning his pants in nervous haste as he quitted a privy. He'd heard the shot. The sound hadn't made his bowels any better.

Lem Gallaghan was next on the scene, via the alley. 'Clegg!' cried Anna, pointing.

The tall man ran, reached the stables. The hostler's boy, confronted by another ranny with a drawn gun, was scared out of his wits. But he managed to point a trembling finger. Gallaghan ran to the edge of the dirt and gazed out at the grasslands in the sun. He shaded his eyes but still couldn't see man or beast. That bastard had a hell of a good start all right.

Gallaghan returned to the little group by the wounded man. Then Sheriff Bestor turned up with an elderly horse-doctor who, it was claimed, was pretty good with humans. The wounded man was carried into a cubbyhole behind a horse set-up.

The doc was quick and efficient. He saw Herb's wound wasn't as bad as it looked – all that red blood an' all. The bulllet, at fairly close range, had gone right through flesh and lost itself, hadn't even touched a bone.

The doc packed the wound, using some salve he'd made himself. Strictly for humankind; too good for hores much as he loved the beasts.

He put the wounded arm in a sling. 'You gotta rest up,' he said. 'So nothin' 'ull turn bad.'

'We were aimin' to come along with you, Trig,' Herb said, his faculties working full-time again. 'Leastways I was.'

'Not without me you weren't,' said his wife tartly.

'You'll have to stay with him now, won't you, gal?' said Sheriff Bestor.

'I know.'

At the meeting place, the *rathskellar*, the bunch had grown. Volunteers. Friends of the owner, half-German, half-Cherokee, some of whom Sheriff Bestor and Loney Dorman also knew. Bestor knew them from their old lawless ways – choosing to forget those for now; Loney knew them from when he, too, had ridden the wild trails.

Some, like the owner, the sheriff's friend, Hans, just hated bandit Jonesy's guts, him and all his boys. Others had more valid reasons for doing so.

One was an ex-friend of Jonesy's whose wife had been raped by two of Jonesy's boys, who had gone unpunished. Another was an Apache whose woman had suffered a like fate, but much worse. They 'spoiled' her, the former brave said. She had run away and now worked in a *bordello* on the other side of the border.

There was a young man called Deke of about the same age as Deputy Prince, whose father had been killed by one of Jonesy's boys. Yet another told an older story of a woman who had fallen in love with a hideout *caballero*, had run off to the hills with him, leaving a husband and boy child behind. He was grown now, a staunch eighteen-year-old who had taught himself to be good with a gun and was eager to capture certain scalps.

And this bunch, never a bunch before, had worthy leaders now, and were willing to follow them through hell and wild waters. A well-known sheriff and his two deputies, one of them a noted *pistolero*, and an old trail-scout, the seemingly ageless Loney.


As he got nearer to the hills and hadn't spotted anybody on his tail, Daley Clegg started in a-thinking again.

He had a thought that he hadn't had before; though in fact he couldn't think why he hadn't had it before. His mind must have been going haywire or something.

That bunch would come to the hideout and, if Gallaghan was with them – and Daley had already figured that the big son-bitch would be – there'd be a chance for Daley to get his revenge *muy pronto*, no waiting, no sweat,

Daley felt like whooping. The ground began to slant upwards under his horse's hooves.

He took what might be called the main trail, though even that was partially hidden and very tortuous. There were two other trails around the periphery of the hills but they were even more difficult to negotiate, as Clegg remembered. For all he knew one might by now be blocked for ever.

He knew that as soon as he reached the more comfortable part of the trail that he was taking he would be watched from above. Jonesy had always had two men watching each approach to his stronghold.

Soon a voice called, 'Hold it right there,' the sound echoing ominously.

He reined in his horse and held his right hand high in the peace signal, though any fool could do that. He took no chances, raised the other hand, balancing in his saddle as best he could. He'd look mighty silly if he fell on his ass!

He shouted, 'My name is Daley Clegg an' I want to see Jonesy. He knows me.'

I might be in a hell of a fix if he didn't know me, Clegg reflected. Or if the big buck takes it in his head to claim that he doesn't know me. You never could tell with Jonesy.

His words had echoed, had been flung back at him as if in mockery.

But the other voice came again and it said, 'Come ahead. Watch yourself.'

So clear and menacing in the quiet air under the sun.

Tentatively, Clegg dropped one hand to his reins, kept the other one half-lifted. He guided his horse slowly forward. Then he saw the man with the rifle, the sun glinting on the steel barrel which was pointed straight at the approaching rider. Then the other man came in sight, to the right of the first marksman and a little to his rear. He had a rifle too.

Getting nearer, Clegg didn't recognize either of them.

It was the second one who guided him; and suddenly the ground began to fall away and the going was easier, the rifleman stepping lively, his weapon still levelled at the rider.

To anybody seeing it for the first time the valley would be a revelation. It had been a revelation for Clegg when he first had sight of it years ago, though he was a man who had never taken much note of his surroundings unless it was important for him to do so.

He thought that the place had been improved considerably since the day he first saw it.

He wouldn't have thought to call the place magical – but that it was.

A wide natural green hollow with a spring causing a thin creek of sweet water to run through the centre of it. Surrounded and hidden by hill and crags, it was a strange, unique freak of nature, the kind that sometimes happened in these wild and savage lands.

A small town had been built here by Jonesy and his minions. A fortress which so far had proved impregnable to attack, though, to be fair, Clegg thought, in this lawless area of the borderlands where law was almost non-existent nobody had tried much. Jonesy took his toll from the various settlements and, in a way, kept other marauders away.

He also ranged wider, however, and brought his booty back to swell his coffers. He had been chased. A couple of times he and his folk had been besieged. But in his valley he was still well-nigh impregnable.

Clegg was led through the buildings, many of them better than those he had left back in the settlement he had recently quitted. Men and women looked at him curiously as they would at any new arrival. A couple of men greeted him by name but didn't change their suspicious looks, for his rifle-toting companion still had the weapon at his back, only lowering it when they reached the biggest log-built building and the robust figure of Jonesy came out on to the wide porch.

He did not speak; he just waited, staring downwards at the new arrival like a hawk watching its prey.

Clegg dismounted and climbed the steps.

He held out his hand and Jonesy took it but did not step aside and lead the visitor into the house.

Clegg said breathlessly (and that wasn't all show), 'A mob is comin' from the settlement. Led by Sheriff Trig Bestor.'

'I remember Bestor,' said Jonesy. He had dropped Clegg's hand as if it was a cold, wet fish.

Clegg plunged on, 'Deputies. Volunteers.' He wasn't sure he was telling the other man the whole truth. He hadn't actually seen that bunch. Still and all . . . .

'Lem Gallaghan,' he added.

'Lem Gallaghan,' Jonesy echoed as if he didn't know whether to believe it or not, his guard down at last, but only momentarily.

'Yeh, Gallaghan,' Clegg said. 'And I want him. He's mine I tell you. He's mine!'

The two men, both with a craziness in their nature, faced each other. Then Jonesy's broad face broke into a grin as he looked down at the smaller man. His blue eyes twinkled as he said, 'Thank you for telling me.'

He could charm a whippoorwill down from a tree, this one, Clegg reflected. He charms the women: how many has he got in his harem here now? But, by Gar, he ain't gonna charm me. I want Gallaghan and I mean to have him.

Had he gone too far in telling Jonesy about Gallaghan? Maybe Gallaghan wouldn't turn up after all. That would be some sort of a hoot all right!

# FIFTEEN

The town marshal did not much like Fat Brackley. But he figured he just couldn't hold the man for the killing of the feller who called himself Bertram Jewell. Couldn't call himself anything else any more. All the evidence pointed to the fact that the killing had been in self-defence as Brackley had claimed. And the old fart of a caretaker at the fat man's building had backed him up.

Brackley was suffering from delayed shock, his doctor said. The fat man seemed to have many friends of an intellectual kind. Brackley shook in his own blubber as he lay abed.

The marshal thought the man might be acting, cunning operator that he was. But Brackley came out of it, though still with a hangdog expression that didn't suit his fat jowls at all. He told the town marshal that he was closing his business in this area and his lawyer, another friend, was seeing to that right now. He said he was going back to Kansas to live with his sister whose husband had recently died.

He might retire then, he said. He had worked hard, he said. At what, thought the marshal mockingly. But he was diplomatic, didn't carp. He would like to put this character's fat ass in jail for a long time. But the slippery cuss had been too smart for that. He can retire his swollen butt completely, the marshal thought, as long as he keeps it out of my jurisdiction – and Kansas was just fine!

He watched the stagecoach bowl away, taking Brackley to the rail-station where the puffin' billy would speed the oily fat man to his new home.

The bunch were approaching a stand of trees and Loney, riding next to the sheriff, was talking animatedly to that worthy. Gallaghan, nearby, thought he had never heard the old coot talk so much all the time he'd known him as he'd talked over the last few days. In some cases, he'd suited his actions to the words.

At the edge of the trees, not yet going round them, Trig Bestor called a halt.

He said, 'Loney tells me that this is the clump of trees before we hit where we're making for. As we are now we can't be spotted by anybody keeping watch at the hideout. Even when we get around the other side of the trees we can't be spotted, unless somebody has a very powerful spy-glass. As we get further on we will be spotted, though, and there won't be much cover from flying lead.'

'It is right what Loney says, señor,' said one of the settlement members of the posse.

'All right. We'll stay in the trees for a mite of time and I'll talk more to Loney and my two deputies.' Finishing his speech, the sheriff moved his horse on and the rest followed.

He halted them again in the shade of the trees and he and Gallaghan, Prince and the old-timer got down from their horses and huddled together. The rest of the bunch dismounted and some of them lit up their last cigarettes before the end of their journey – and who would know what would happen then?

Soon Bestor called them together. He was smoking a cigarette, as were his two deputies. Loney contented himself with a villainous-looking pipe and tobacco that gave off a pungent smoke.

'Signals,' said one wag. 'They'll think the Injuns are comin' an' run for their lives.' But nobody laughed.

'Listen,' snapped Trig Bestor. 'There are three ways o' getting to that hideout. But one of 'em is a bad one. Loney thinks in fact that that one might be blocked by now. He thinks, however, that, no matter what, he can find a way. So him an' Gallaghan an' Prince are goin' on ahead of us – I'm gonna give 'em fifteen minutes,' he consulted a heavy gun-metal half-hunter, 'before we ride in straight, ride in fast; faster still if we hear shots, whether they're Loney's signal or shots from the other side.'

He paused, looking at the men around him, a sweeping glance before he pronounced, 'Anybody who wants to pull back can do that now an' nobody 'ull think the worse of 'em.'

111

There were murmurs. But it seemed that nobody wanted to move in the opposite direction. And the three men who had been picked for the first go-down left the rest on the trail and veered off in a slanting line.

Looking back a while later, they could still see the trees. But then the distance put them out of sight and the craggy sides of the hills were in front of them. Gallaghan and Prince were letting Loney lead the way now and he seemed to know where he was going, slowing though he did from time to time, peering at the ground, gazing at the now-tortuous terrain about him.

'Should be around here someplace,' he said. 'I reckon this prickly bush has spread a lot since I was here last.'

They didn't ask him how long that had been; but Gallaghan said, 'It grows like wildfire, sure.'

'Talkin' about fire,' Loney was a little ahead again and he pointed. 'Look at that.' Thorn thickets had been burned to ashes and powder and now new green shoots were fighting to spring through.

Whether the sun had been responsible for the firing or whether it had been started by human hands was hard to determine. But the flames had not spread as far as the three men had at first thought, they had obviously either petered out or been doused with water, even rain maybe.

Loney brought his horse to a dead stop. 'That's it,' he said hoarsely. Gallaghan and Prince followed the direction of his gaze. They had both been amazed as they had travelled; and they were being surprised again by their awareness of the quality of the old man's eyesight.

The section of jagged rock at which the three of them gazed now was like a spiked and perilous wall.

'That's it,' said the oldster again. 'That's where the old trail started, and a bitch of a one it was I'll tell you.'

Prince said, 'Looks like there was a fall and it was left, blocked. And the brush grew and somebody set fire to it hoping to clear the trail again. But they couldn't make it.'

'Maybe we can,' Loney said, and he sounded as if he meant every word.

'I guess we can try,' said Gallaghan.

Prince said, 'Pity we didn't bring some sort of digging tools.'

Loney said, ' I don't think they would've been much good, son. Them rocks are close together, they'll have to be shifted by bare hands.' He was already getting down from his horse, and he was as quick as the other two.

Dougal lay in a cave. His feet were not tied but they were bare. His hands were tied behind his back. He lay on his side on the hard floor in a position he had found the most comfortable – and that wasn't saying much.

He had been watered and fed, not too badly. Evidently Jonesy didn't aim to hang him yet. Maybe the big feller had more interesting plans, better entertainment for the folks. If so, no doubt the moustached, dwarfish Rigona would have a hand in that, him and his goddamn whip.

113

Dougal had tried to work on his bonds, rubbing them on the hard floor, but without any great success. The floor was too flat, and covered with sand that had sifted from above.

He had crawled around the walls, using his feet as levers. The walls were almost as smooth as glass. No jagged pieces. No bump of any use. Dougal wondered how old the cave was. Prehistoric maybe.

It was empty but it smelled musty as if goods had been kept here at some time, furs or pelts maybe. Had hunters once used this strange valley? Were there any more caves? These folk certainly didn't live in caves. They lived in smart ex-army tents, in shacks, in houses like the one Jonesy had, though his was the first of all of course, the biggest and the best.

They had the stream and even some vegetable gardens, tended by the women. Dougal had seen a few cows. When they were used up the boys could steal others. They brought provisions in from outside – booze and the better things.

It's a fine place to die in, Dougal thought sardonically.

The light was momentarily blocked as the Mexican girl came into the cave. She had brought him food before. Now she had coffee in a can. She smiled at him. Her dark eyes mocked him. Was she looking forward to the ceremony which would take him out of her sight for ever?

She hadn't spoken to him. She hadn't threatened him. She hadn't mocked him with anything but her eyes. Maybe she even had a yen for him: the last comforts of a man about to die.

He pulled himself into a sitting position against the wall and grinned at her. 'Cut me loose, honah,' he said.

She pursed her lips. Then she said something in her own language. He didn't understand it. She held the coffee-can to his lips and he took the hot, sweet liquid, which was good. Could he use his feet, leg her over?

But he couldn't do anything with his hands as his wrists were lashed so tightly together that the rawhide brought scalding pain if he tried to manipulate it.

Some of the coffee spilled down on to his shirt-front. The girl laughed huskily. A mocking sound.

But maybe there was hope for him yet. He watched her as she moved away with the empty coffee-can. She was limned against the light. Her legs were fine, slightly bowed. Her buttocks rotated smoothly, swaying provocatively. She passed out of his sight. The valley sounds came through to him and bars of sunlight slanted across the mouth of the cave.

There was a girl locked in a tiny cabin which was empty but smelled of some kind of sour fruit, a smell she couldn't identify. She had been fed and now she was waiting.

She was brown-skinned and petite and her name was Ruth. It was not her real name. She couldn't remember her real name. She had been rechristened Ruth by Anna and Herb Pickett who had been like mother and father to her. She wondered what had happened to them. The uncertainty was like an ache in her heart. But she was fatalistic: it was in her nature to be so.

She was waiting for the little man. The one they called Rigona. The one with the whip. Fleetingly, she wondered what had happened to the big man, the one that Rigona had put down with that cruel whip. Were he by any chance here in this strange place, she thought, he would try to save her. But it was a remote possibility. Maybe he was dead.

She had no hope.

She waited.

# SIXTEEN

Prince said, 'Surely some of the gang could've moved this lot, used crowbars, picks, things like that.'

Loney said, 'They don't like hard work. I heard that Jonesy was puttin' on some weight hisself.'

Gallaghan said, 'I'm inclined to think that Jonesy, after reflectin' on it, decided that the blockage should be left like this, no men needed to guard a third trail, and that a mighty rough one.'

Loney said, 'You could be right.'

Gallaghan didn't seem to hear him now, was looking back at his horse, the big one he called Rip. 'He wants to help,' the big man mused. 'I've got some rope in my war-bag.'

He moved towards the horse who backed skittishly. 'I don't want to play,' said his master. 'C'mere, yuh irritating cayuse.'

The horse stopped, turned his head away a little, watched Gallaghan out of the corner of one eye and, when the man reached him, showed his teeth. But then

117

he quit the game and let Gallaghan do what he wanted to do.

A rope on the cantle, the other end on a big rock and, at command, the big, powerful horse pulling with all his might.

'It's comin',' said Prince. 'It's comin'.'

The big rock was sliding, bringing smaller ones with it.

The obstruction was becoming loosened. Trickles of small stones, and powdery dust and shale were coming down. And Rip, resting, snorting with breathless satisfaction.

The men worked. They paused, Loney was coughing thinly.

They wiped their dirt-smeared, sweating faces. They had a way to go yet.

Loney, his coughing fit over, asked, 'Do you remember the freak storms they had down here a while back, the river runnin' wild an' some of the lower ground getting flooded?'

The other two said they remembered all right, and the old one went on, 'The rain could've loosened these rocks – an' the water gone on running down the hill, down the trail, if there's any of it left.'

The others agreed: Yeh, that was likely.

Gallaghan said, 'The hoss helped as well.' He turned. 'Let's try it again, boy.'

Ruth heard a commotion outside, shouting voices of men, the shrill voices of women, the female scum of the borderlands. The dark girl's pretty lips curled. But she went to the tiny, grimy window and, after craning her head this and that way, managed to look out.

A man, his hands behind his back, was being dragged to the lower centre of the green valley. A jeering crowd was following. The two men who were dragging the other man reached their destination. A tall, stout stake, a pillar of wood. A picture flitted across Ruth's mind, a picture from long ago . . . .

A man tied to a burning stake as she watched from a concealed place. And that man had been her father. She did not know what had happened to her mother. She did not know who the people had been who had burned her father alive. And his screams had seemed like something from another world.

A missing child who was found, succoured.

The image died. She watched the scene outside. The man was tied to the stake. She saw Rigona and his whip. So the little man would not be visiting her yet.

Her view was blocked out by jostling bodies. The entertainment was about to begin. But then the big man, Jonesy, appeared and the ranks parted and Ruth had another glimpse of the man at the stake and Rigona facing him, the wicked thong of his whip curling at his feet.

The leader had arrived. There was a ragged cheer and then the sound died. Ruth even heard the first crack of the whip. And she flinched as if the cruel lash had torn her own soft flesh. There was a great 'Aaa-aah' from the crowd. Ruth turned away from the window, went and sat in a corner the furthest away from the window that she could get.

They hit the trail and began to climb. It was hard going. From time to time they had to stop, work again moving obstacles that blocked their path.

Before leaving the horses, knowing they couldn't possibly get them through this tortuous terrain, they had grabbed their canteens. They had laved their faces with water and taken a swig each. They had checked their weapons. Between them they had enough fire-power to take on an army, were it not too big. They figured they could depend on Trig Bestor and the rest of the posse to be there when things got really rough.

They all had rifles, figured that in the first go-down they'd need those long, shining weapons which certainly made a man feel good.

Vines and prickly plants clutched at them, bit at them. Their lips moved as they swore softly. They tried not to waste too much breath. But there were times when a man just had to cuss.

They used their knives here and there to cut their way through. Gallaghan had the best knife of all: the other two admired it.

They hit a crest and still could not see anything inter-esting ahead of them. But, downhill now, the going became a mite easier.

A sound reached them and they paused.

'A mob,' said Gallaghan. 'Sounds like they're havin' a party.'

Loney said, 'I hope the other boys ain't got there too soon.'

'They won't have,' said young Prince, staunchly.

'Take it easy,' said Loney. He was beginning to limp a bit. 'Take it slow an' keep a-lookin'.'

But, after all, they burst in upon the scene suddenly. And they raised their rifles and started shooting, picking their targets methodically: the men who turned towards them in shock, already somewhat demoralized by the sudden vision of these figures, advancing, spewing death.

The Indian who rode with the posse belonged to the ranks of those greatest guerrilla fighters of all, the Apaches. He left his horse and went ahead on foot, climbing away from the trail.

He got the first sentry with a knife, slitting his throat. But there had been a small sound and the other man, himself half-Indian, caught it and turned. The Apache aimed straight, got the man in the head, killing him instantly.

Shots had been heard already from the valley. The attacking force, all on foot by then, moved more swiftly, the horses following them, ready for further use.

The Apache rejoined them, grinning savagely as only an Apache can after pulling off a coup.

First blood to him. He wanted more. These pigs had 'spoiled' his wife.

They climbed upwards. Then they were over the knob of the hill and starting to go down, the progress smoother, faster, here and there soft grass under their feet.

The gunfire ahead of them was getting fiercer. They redoubled their efforts.

They broke out into the open quite suddenly and looked down on the tight township in the green expanse spread out below, a sight that most of them had never seen before. They moved on, in spaced groups.

Gallaghan, Prince and Loney had gotten themselves ensconced in cover not far from the narrow entrance to the old trail they had come through.

The bigger man of the three was behind a boulder which looked as if it had fallen from the skies above. The younger deputy was fairly near, on his belly behind a slab of rock that seemed to have grown up out of the ground, a natural table-top ready for a picnic under the sun and shaded by the craggy slopes behind which the sun was going down. The oldster, who was using a Sharps rifle as if he was still in his buffalo-hunting days, had a stand (that was what they used to call them) behind a pile of stones that looked as if they had been specially placed there for his protection.

Women were running for cover, screaming. Nobody molested them. Male bodies lay in the grass. A ranny with a red bandanna round his head was making mewling animal noises as he attempted to crawl. There was dust in the air and the gunsmoke was drifting.

Men had taken cover in buildings and behind walls trying to pick off the attackers who had come so suddenly from the disused back trail, appearing like ghosts from the rocks themselves.

The new attackers sought cover, were able to do so without mishap as their arrival was almost as much a surprise to the camp as the onslaught of the first visitors had been.

More visitors with death in their hearts.

There had been lethargic times in the encampment. There had been no big jobs. The men had dallied with the women. Jonesy had had a time with two pretty *señoritas* visiting from over the big river.

The surprise onslaught, coming first from a direction from which it had been least expected, had had a demoralizing effect; attacked from behind as most of the populace had been while watching the entertainment arranged by Jonesy, and put on by the prisoner who called himself Dougal, and by Rigona and his whip.

That Rigona: he was a caution all right!

Some of the men hadn't even brought any weapons out with them, hadn't believed they needed them. Some of them were shot down as they ran for cover and their weapons, which they never reached. Their bodies lay in the dust. The attackers were merciless. It was as if they were destroying lice. As far as the voluntary posse from the settlement was concerned, they were wiping out years of insults and demands and frustrations.

# SEVENTEEN

Gallaghan went down on one knee. A bullet zipped over his head. He thumbed the hammer of his gun, speeding a slug on its way to bury itself in the skull of the man who had used him as a target and hadn't made it, would never have another chance at anything.

Half-rising, the big feller heard a sound behind. A scream? He jerked his head around. The sound had come from a small hut, the door of which was half open.

Beyond that open door a woman was screaming: the sound was dominant now even above the gunfire and the other clamour. The sound was piercing.

Gallaghan straightened to his full length. Gun in hand, he ran forward, burst through the door, swinging it wide with his shoulder, instinctively half-crouching as he did this.

A man had a girl back against the opposite wall. The girl's face appeared over the man's shoulder. Eyes wide, mouth open. Gallaghan remembered that face. The pretty brown-skinned face of the girl from the Picketts' place, the girl who had been kidnapped.

The man's identity was established too, a small man, turning, reaching. The twisted, moustached, dark face of the one called Rigona.

In two more long strides Gallaghan reached him, grabbed him, lifted him, the drawn gun falling from the little man's fist and him squealing like a pig. The big man swung him half-around and flung him at the window which shattered with the impact, showering the glass.

Rigona was small. But the window was small also, and narrow. The body got stuck. The body's legs kicked a few times, then became still.

Gallaghan turned to the girl who was pulling her torn bodice across herself, covering herself.

'Stay here, honah. I'll lock the door. Wait for me.'

She nodded her head, her hair tumbling. 'Thank you,' she said.

He did as he had said. Then he turned to the man in the window.

Rigona's face was slashed and bloody. His head was at an awkward sideways angle, his eyes staring sightlessly, his teeth bared. It was evident that his neck had been broken and he was quite dead.

Sheriff Bestor was in the centre of something that now looked like a sort of arena. He was by a stake where a body hung, slumped, still.

Gallaghan ran over, saw the state of the body of the staked man, the blood, the threaded remnants of what had once been a checked shirt.

The head was slumped on the mutilated breast. Trig Bestor caught hold of the head by the thick black hair and lifted it so that the face was revealed: the contorted dead face of the young killer who had called himself Dougal.

There was a hole in the dead man's temple from which a thin trickle of blood had escaped.

'I was after him,' Gallaghan said.

'No need any more,' said Trig. 'The job you wanted to do has been done for you. A stray bullet I guess.'

The bandits were being besieged in their buildings, their nooks and crannies and hidey-holes. The area around the two big lawmen was fairly clear, except for human detritus.

Then Gallaghan's head jerked upwards, became fixed, as he spotted something. His eyes became flint-like, his jaw hardened.


Daley Clegg was about to make his escape when, suddenly, Jonesy barred his way.

The big gang-leader's eyes were full of fury. 'You brought them here,' he stormed.

'I didn't, bucko. I swear I didn't.'

'They followed you . . .' Jonesy was becoming inarticulate. A line of white foam formed on his lips and his eyes were thin, the eyes of a crazy man. There was a gun in his hand. He raised it.

Clegg shot from the hip, the muzzle of his gun tilted upwards. The range was close. The target was unmissable for a gun-artiste like Clegg who wasn't as mad as Jonesy. Only nearly.

The bullet went through Jonesy's mouth and upwards and took part of the top of his head off before whining thinly away.

Gallaghan was running. Clegg saw him, a sudden thing, flung a shot at him and missed, turned, scuttled. He had run his string. There was too much now for him to handle.

Nearest to him was the old trail which had been uncovered by Gallaghan, Prince and Loney. Clegg took that trail. There was cover. But he had to get a horse!

Gallaghan glanced down at the body as he passed it. There was nothing he could do for his old saddle-pard. Nothing he would have wanted to do.

All a long time ago . . . .

This wasn't the Jonesy he had known.

This was a dead thing now, and that had been inevitable. It had had to happen, but, sneakingly, Gallaghan was glad that it hadn't happened at his hand.

He flung himself forward into the rocks at the base of the old trail, the rocks that had sheltered him when he first entered this place.

A bullet narrowly missed him. Then he heard Clegg running again, scrambling, his boot-heels thudding.

The sounds behind were like mocking echoes.

On the other side of the valley, at the main trail, the horses of the posse were being moved in. Men on horses would have been easier targets. For the main attack the posse had come in on foot. That ploy,

127

combined with the ghoulish preoccupation enjoyed by the denizens of the stronghold, had worked like an evil charm, a turnabout.

Taking chances, Gallaghan climbed as fast as he could up the narrow, old trail. But his quarry, it seemed, had quit shooting, was just trying his hardest to escape. Still, the pursuer knew that he would have to watch himself mightily when he broke out at the mouth of the trail. He went up and over; and then he was going down again.

He had almost reached the bottom and was scrambling among small boulders, sand and shale when he heard a horse breaking into a gallop ahead of him. He broke cover, his gun lifted.

He stopped dead. Clegg was escaping in the saddle of one of the three horses that had been left waiting here, browsing. And the horse that the man had taken was the fastest: Gallaghan's big bay, Rip.

Clegg had put spurs to him, no doubt.

And that cayuse was going like the wind!

Gallaghan came out into the open. He wasn't aiming to risk a shot. He put two fingers into his mouth and emitted a piercing whistle. Then another one.

Rip stopped dead in his tracks. He was giving the strange rider a run; but now the signal, one of the many that his genial master had taught him! And that signal – two blasts – meant *Stop*.

The rider, jerked abruptly in the saddle, had a fight to stay there, barely made it – but did. He rowelled the horse savagely, but to no avail. And, dammit, the beast was turning around!

Nothing else for it! Clegg got down from the saddle.

Gallaghan was striding forward. Clegg turned towards him, waited. Neither of the men yet had a gun out in sight.

Clegg spread his legs and leaned his body forward a little in a half-crouch. He moved his arms, held his clawed hands away from his body. A classic gunfighter's stance.

'Take me, bucko,' he shouted.

Gallaghan didn't reply, kept coming.

He halted at a reasonable length from his man and adopted a similar stance, though his was somewhat more upright.

'Reach then,' he said, his voice almost a whisper.

'Damn you,' snarled Clegg, and he moved.

He was fast. He was very fast.

His gun had cleared its holster when Gallaghan, his gun held almost at arm's length (he had been *that* fast) bucked for the first time. But Clegg had leaned sideways a bit – it was a trick he'd used before and men had died because of it – and Gallaghan's bullet only caught him in the shoulder. But it spun him. Then, as he fought to regain his equilibrium and raise his gun again at the same time, the other man's second bullet hit him.

It got him full in the breastbone and flung him backwards as if he had been punched by a giant fist.

His legs kicked up. He hit the ground with the back of his head and his legs stretched out, the toes of his boots pointing at the sky, at the dying red sun.

The body became still.

The horse called Rip had backed off a little. He had heard gunfire before but still didn't much like it. He came forward now and looked down curiously at the dead man.

'C'mon, boy,' Gallaghan said.

The horse trotted forward, head tilted at a quizzical angle.

'You're a smart one,' the man said. 'I ought to put you in a circus.'

The horse showed his teeth in a grin as if he had understood the words and didn't believe any of them. The man mounted him and they made for the entrance to the old trail.

The horse didn't look back. Neither did the man.

A dishevelled, unarmed man ran into the horse and rider on the old trail, was forced back by them. A few of the bandits had escaped through one or other of the more easily accessible exits from the valley. Loney and Prince, coming down the old trail to collect their horses, greeted Deputy Gallaghan and his prisoner, said they'd see 'em again pretty soon.

There were captives. And there were those who would never move again. There was talk of burning all the buildings to the ground. Then one of the members of the posse said that the townsfolk could come here and take the places apart, the lumber would come in mighty handy.

Trig Bestor said that was all right by him: he had prisoners to handle and transport. They were roped

130

together. Since they were out of his jurisdiction, Trig had to find nearer law, didn't aim to transport prisoners all the way to his own bailiwick anyway, no sirree.

Lem Gallaghan said, 'I've got more lone riding to do.'

He did however return with the rest to the settlement and take the girl called Ruth back to her people, Anna and Herb Pickett.

Herb's wounded shoulder was mending well. He and his wife and the girl elected to ride with Gallaghan, back with him, hoped he would bide a while at their place.

# EIGHTEEN

As a matter of courtesy, and the fact that he actually liked the people, Gallaghan stopped over at the Pickett's place for a meal. They were comparatively new friends, but very good ones. He knew that he would pay them a visit again when he had the time – if he was lucky enough (or good enough) to be able to make the time.

There was something he had to finish, put an end to. Only there was a fleeting thought in his mind that it might put an end to *him*.

He had to do what he had to do, and that was the be-all and end-all of it.

He'd been lucky so far, oh yeh!

The Picketts – and their brown-skinned girl who, luckily, had come to no harm, bade him a fond so-long and Anna and Ruth kissed him and stood waving till he couldn't see them any more.

He had not bothered the two females about his worries but, as a form of courtesy had, on the side, told

Herb about some of them. Herb had elected to come along with him, as had Prince and Loney. He had to track down the rest of the people – the man or men – who had been responsible for the death of his old friend Christopher, expunge the grief of Chris's sister Julie and the boy Jonathon.

He figured it was his job and his alone. He gratefully, courteously but with gentle firmness turned down any offers of help in his quest which could, he knew, turn out to be a long one.

He had no time to lose. He knew he had to visit Julie first to see how she and her son were faring. His friend and colleague Trig had told him of Julie's and Jonathon's trouble with Daley Clegg (the *late* Daley Clegg). Delightedly, Gallaghan had figured he'd like to hear the tale himself – from the lips of two of the protagonists. It was as good an excuse as any to justify a visit to Julie and Jonathon.

By the time they got there he and Rip both needed a rest, and some sustenance.

The two individuals were mighty glad to see him. Julie kissed him, and it was more than a friendly peck. She held him, her lovely eyes full of tears of relief.

She said, 'You big lunk, I'm so glad to see you all in one piece.' And then she started to laugh through her tears, and Jonathon moved delightedly around them and Gallaghan turned to him and said, 'You did good, bucko.'

'I did my best,' Jonathon said.

Then they sat at the kitchen table and had coffee and

biscuits while the woman bustled about making a proper meal for the returning man. And the boy told the story, his mother interjecting bits from time to time. Then the boy said to the man, 'I've got something to show you,' and left the table.

He returned with it in his fist, something that looked like a log, or chunk of round firewood. It was that. But the boy had wrapped rawhide around the slimmer end of it and painted this improvised handle with black paint, now dried to a glossy finish.

'This is what I whacked him with,' he said. 'I'm keeping it as a souvenir.'

He handed the weapon to the laughing big feller who weighed it in his hand, made a practice swipe.

'Put some leather on it an' hang it on the wall,' he said.

'That' a good idea,' Jonathon said.

His mother said, 'I don't know whether I'd like to keep looking at it.'

It was left hanging in the air, not the club but the question of what was to be done with it; so Jonathon put it back in the drawer from which he'd taken it.

In all this Julie's only regret was that she no longer had the friendship of the neighbouring sisters, Dru and Caroley who, through some sort of misguided loyalty, had set Daley Clegg free.

Oh, they'd tried to make amends afterwards, directing Sheriff Bestor; but that did not alter the fact that they, and nobody else, had set a crazy killer loose again.

The girl touched the scar on the man's forehead and

said, 'I've been wondering about this and didn't like to ask. But now I can't help myself.'

Gallaghan told her, softening the gory details, said he didn't even have a headache now.

The day was lengthening. He had to ride.

'Brackley,' the town marshal said. 'He's gone. After he killed a man. Self-defence. I had to let him go. Killed a feller called hisself Bertram Jewell, called hisself a range detective. We buried him. No kin far as we could find out. I guess Brackley used him for somep'n an' then they fell out.'

'Where'd Brackley go?' Gallaghan asked.

'Back to Kansas to live with his sister, as he said. She's a widow, so he says, she'll look after him. Says he's gonna retire. I don't think the man's all that well now, not that I'm gonna bother my skull about that.'

'Me neither,' said Gallaghan sardonically. 'But I've got to get to that fat man before he dies on me, I tell you that.'

'Maybe the telegraph office got a line on him,' the marshal said.

'Yeh, thanks, partner, I'll try them.'

Gallaghan tried them and, to his surprise, came up trumps. He hit the trail again.

He rode some, then caught a train, putting Rip in the car at the back. The horse didn't seem too pleased, showed his teeth. However, when his master went to get him out at the end of the journey he was contentedly munching hay in the company of a pretty little brown filly and was reluctant to leave her.

But duty called. He kicked his heels a bit, but then settled down to his usual long-legged lope which would soon turn into a merry gallop if he had the sign. But his master didn't give him that sign, was soon gazing at a house in the town that had been their destination.

Eventually Rip was tied to a white picket-fence outside a small but bright flower garden.

Gallaghan walked up a narrow, sanded path, climbed on to a narrow, neat veranda and rapped with his knuckles on a door painted chocolate brown.

He waited, hearing no sound from inside.

He looked at those windows that were in his sight. No curtains moved. He looked back at the garden, at the horse who was peering at him enquiringly over the white fence.

Rip's ears pricked, then he lowered his head again, had obviously found something he could chew.

Gallaghan knocked at the door again. No answer.

He grasped the knob, exerted pressure which he discovered wasn't needed. The wooden globe turned easily in his fingers.

He pushed the door. It creaked slightly as it opened, but there was no other sound.

He called, 'Hallo. Anybody there?'

Silence of the grave.

Almost opposite him was another door that was almost open. He paced across to this, knocked upon it and called out 'Hallo' once more.

Still no reply.

He eased the door open, eased himself through. Almost immediately he saw Brackley.

The fat man, who was in no condition to receive any visitor, lay across a plain *chaise-longue* in his shirtsleeves. The ruffled front of his white shirt was marred by a red patch.

Gallaghan strode forward and dropped on one knee before the still form.

He felt for a pulse and, at least, found one. But it was very weak.

He heard a sound behind him, from the direction of the outer door. He quickly took out his deputy's badge from his vest pocket and pinned it on his chest.

He met the small elderly lady in the hall. She looked startled; but she was quickly reassured by the tall, handsome young man with a silver star on his breast, who said, 'I came to see your brother, ma'am. He has been attacked, needs a doctor immediately.'

Her hand went involuntarily to her mouth and her pale-blue eyes widened with shock. But she was of staunch frontier stock, no doubt about that. She quickly recovered herself and said, 'There's a doctor right next door, I'll go fetch him.'

She was a comely woman as quick on the uptake as her brother who had never been an amateur at quick thinking. She went back through the door. Gallaghan noted that she had already placed her few packages against the wall. She went through the other door, back to Brackley and, to his surprise saw that the fat bulk was stirring slightly. Gallaghan went down on one knee again. In a sort of praying position, he reflected sardon-ically.

Brackley's eyes opened slowly but did not focus prop-erly.

The tall, younger man said, ' It's me. Gallaghan. Who did this to you?'

The eyes blinked; the lips moved, quivered.

The words came very slowly, haltingly. Like a child learning to talk.

'He did it . . . the young man with the eye-glasses.'

What did he mean?

*Who* did he mean?

The woman came back with a tall silver-haired man. Gallaghan quickly introduced himself. But the doctor was more concerned with the patient; who lay still, eyes closed again.

'I don't think he should be moved yet.' The doctor turned to the woman. 'Martha, will you call young Clay for me?'

'I will, Amos.' She bustled away.

'Clay's my assistant,' the doctor explained.

'I found Brackley like this,' said Gallaghan. 'I didn't see anybody. I guess now I ought to go see the local law.'

'I guess so, Deputy,' said the man called Amos.

It was a small Kansas cowtown with trusting people. And a fat sheriff who was shocked but not hurried, seemed lazy and somewhat phlegmatic also. He looked slightly interested, though, when the visitor mentioned a young man with eye-glasses.

'Saw a feller answered to that description. A couple

o' times. Looked like an Easterner, dressed that way. Smart. What do you call it? – dapper. Yeh. Last time I saw him he was coming out of the telegraph office down the street.'

So they went to the office and, much to his delighted surprise, the visiting lawman got an address. He told a bit more of his story to the local law.

'I once knew Trig Bestor,' the man said, but didn't elaborate. 'I've heard o' you too, Gallaghan. To do, I think, with the bunch that were called the Kansas Riders. You knew them?'

'Some,' said Gallaghan.

'You know Kansas purty well then?'

'Some,' said Gallaghan.

'That address, that's outa my jurisdiction.'

'Mine too,' said Gallaghan. He took his star off and put it back in his vest pocket.

He went back along town. Maybe Brackley would be able to tell him some more now. It was an abject hope. He was confronted by a weeping woman, a stern-faced doctor, and a younker in a white apron who looked kind of bewildered.

Brackley was dead. 'I thought . . .' the tall, silver-haired man's voice tailed off, then went on more softly, 'but his heart couldn't stand it.'

'He died peaceably,' the younker said.

'I've got a line on who I think killed him,' said the big deputy.

He didn't stay long after that and, after he'd left, Doc Amos said to his old friend Martha, who had been his own dead wife's old classmate, 'There's something implacable about that man. I think your brother will ultimately be avenged, Martha.'

The rotund local sheriff was there right then and he had no comment to make, puffing on an evil-smelling stogie, blowing derisive clouds of smoke.

Gallaghan, riding then, might not have agreed wholly with the doctor's pungent remarks. He could call himself an educated man now, could the big deputy, yanked himself up by his bootstraps as he had surely done, particularly in more recent years. He knew what the word 'implacable' meant.

But at the moment he wasn't too sure about anything yet or what he might do about it if he did. Maybe he was less implacable now than he had been all the while through this long trail, the raids, the killings.

But he was pondering, as he often did while he was in the saddle atop ol' Rip, who wasn't old at all, not in any manner of means.

*Questions.* Had Fat Brackley really meant to retire as he had told the town marshal back home? Had he really meant to stay with his sister, live with her? Or had his scheming brain decided that there were other fish to fry? Had he by devious means tracked down the person or persons who had paid for the two boys – Dougal and Armitage – to kill three men, thus bringing about the mistaken, mocking death of Lem Gallaghan's friend, Christopher Dakes?

So much to find yet, Gallaghan thought, as he rode steadily. Not too far: that was a telling factor. But, whatever Brackley had wanted, he wasn't about to get it now.

So much to find out yet.

Still and all, maybe the close-mouthed fat man had, in the end, partly vindicated himself.

The way was becoming strangely familiar. Changed here and there maybe, but awakening memory-echoes in the fertile mind of the big man on horseback.

The name of a town too. A small town, though it would perhaps have grown larger in the passing years. A town on the other side of Dodge City.

# NINETEEN

He had contemplated taking a train for part of the way. But he knew Rip wouldn't like that. The big bay couldn't expect to find a nice filly waiting for him in every caboose.

Anyway ol' Rip was goin' fine, as happy as an inebriated lark.

They approached Dodge by the cutting that had been dubbed the Western Trail. It wasn't the first time the man had been along there, though, as he remembered, on another horse. Coming *back* too; *fast*. But, now, that seemed a hell of a long time ago.

The man did not look for landmarks, did not choose to awaken memories. He was still young in this wild land that could make a man seem old before his time.

The last few days had wearied him, had wearied his spirit. He wanted the whole thing to be over. But, then, he didn't particularly want to remember the wild young sprig that he had been when he'd ridden the Western Trail before.

And now the landmarks were becoming dim, the shadows long. Then the night fell suddenly as it did in these parts. Rip was spryer than ever. And then Gallaghan saw the lights like a parade of stars.

There seemed more of them than there used to be. Well, there would be, he told himself.

He rode into the main street and lights were all around him. He slowed Rip, looking around him, trying to get his bearings.

There was a queue outside a place which blazed with light, seemed to be a theatre. Men and women jostled. The street erupted in noise. A man staggered out of the queue as another man hit him, a woman screaming in protest.

A big man, fists whirling, chasing a staggering smaller man. A screaming woman wielding a closed parasol, beating the big man across the head with it so that he, too, began to stagger, turn clumsily, shouting abuse, clutching at the woman, who eluded him with a little skip and jump. She was no filly, but she was fast.

A man shouted. A man came down the street, burly, wearing an officious-looking black vest and, rather incongruously, a brown derby four-square on his bullet head. One of those fellers who are called constables, Gallaghan reflected.

He carried a truncheon, and he strode forward and hit the other big feller, the bullying one, across the back of the head with this. The bully fell heavily, raising a small cloud of dust. The street here wasn't any better than those in most Western townships, cart-rutted, hoof-pocked, dry with powder that got up a man's nose till the rains came.

The constable waved the woman and her small paramour back into the queue, the truculent hen fussing over her chick. The constable grabbed the unconscious bully by the back of his collar and dragged him down the street. A few folks in the queue cheered. Nobody else seemed to take much notice. The two men disappeared into a convenient alley. Maybe the jailhouse was up there. Gallaghan couldn't remember one in an alley. Maybe the constable wanted to try out his truncheon some more.

Gallaghan rode slowly onwards. The sound of a fife and kettledrum sounded behind him and he turned his head. The music came from inside the big shack that looked like a theatre. The folk were filing in there now. A man appeared with a tall pole, a notice atop it. THE MAGIC SHOW.

Gallaghan passed a place he thought he recognized. Half hotel, half bawdyhouse. A false front which looked like it might collapse into the street at any moment, had looked like that for years. It would have a space at the back and struts holding the towering edifice upright. Maybe even a windbreak right back and, in between, a picnic area in benign days. 'Picnic', that was a funny word, Gallaghan reflected. The only picnic (if you could call it that) he could remember was on hard ground before a smoky fire behind a chuck wagon.

He was getting his bearings now, steered Rip into a

narrower street which, however, was as well-lit as the main one.

His destination was approximately half-way down this street. A place that was more of a gambling house than a conventional saloon. He hitched the bay at a narrow hitching rail; but there was hay and a small water trough. The big bay would be fine for a while, was already eyeing neighbourly nags with interest.

'Don't start anything, bucko,' Gallaghan warned him and turned and shouldered through the batwings.

Things came back to him in a colourful rush. The place hadn't changed much!

The green baize table, the roulette wheel, the narrow bar with the half-naked girl in a boat, no other painting like it in any other place like this that Gallaghan had known.

The dais in the middle of the floor with the look-out man perched there in his chair. The steps which Gallaghan was about to pass now.

From above him a courteous voice asked, 'Can I help you, suh?'

Gallaghan halted, looked up at the young man on the dais who had a long-barrelled Colt on his knee. A handsome black-haired young buck with a white-teethed smile but eyes that were keen and challenging.

Gallaghan said, 'I'm lookin' for Buff. I'm an old friend of his. Is he still here?'

'He surely is,' said the look-out boy. He turned away, said to a somebody that Gallaghan could not see, 'Go get Buff, Perce. A friend of his wants to see him.'

He turned back to Gallaghan. 'All right, suh?' The calculating eyes. The Southern-flavoured voice which reminded the big man suddenly of the late Jonesy.

'All right.'

But then another voice cut in. Buff had been quick. He hadn't changed any more than his establishment had. He still limped, still moved with his big head thrust forward – threateningly almost – because of the twisted back which made him less tall than he used to be.

Buff had been a rodeo clown till a wild bull fell on him. He had earned big money, though, from his dangerous antics, and had bought this colourful establishment which kept him good.

'By all that's holy,' he boomed. 'How've you been, you ol' bastard?'

'Not so old as you, pizen,' said Gallaghan as his hand was engulfed by a paw bigger than his own.

The young man on the dais was looking down at them. Buff raised his shaggy head and said, 'This is Lem Gallaghan, Paul. He had your job up there once upon a time.'

The younker called Paul reached a hand down and Gallaghan took it.

'I remember Buff told me about you, Mr Gallaghan.' There was no searching look in the dark eyes now. So young, thought the big man with a little pang, and obviously very good at what he did – or the shrewd Buff wouldn't have hired him in the first place.

'Come back to the office, Lem,' the hunchbacked man said and he led the way.

146

Buff had done a lot of listening. Now it was his turn to talk.

'Name's Rafe Tringle. Works for Lucken who runs the big ranch on a ways.'

Gallaghan said, 'Burt Lucken who used to be a preacher-man before he started to run beef?'

'The same. Say, Lem, didn't you work for him for a while?'

'Yeh, about twelve months. Sort of straw boss. Didn't suit me. He was a good man to work for, though, Sort of adopted me, y'know.'

''S'funny you used the word adopted, Lem. Lucken sort of adopted Tringle I guess, though he already had a son of his own.'

'Young Lenny. I remember him as a boy.'

'Lenny's dead, Lem.' Buff ploughed on before the big man could interrupt again. 'But Rafe Tringle wandered into the ranch one night half-starved, sick. He's been there ever since. I know him. I never trusted him, allus thought there was somep'n strange about him . . . .'

But Gallaghan got his question in. 'What happened to Lenny?'

'Four men hit the bank in town. Cyprus End, y'know. Not far from the ranch.'

'I know.'

'Lenny was there, took a hand. They shot him dead. The ol' bank guard had been down the street, was

coming back. He got one of 'em, stone dead. But that
didn't bring young Lenny back. The other three sons-a-
bitches got clean away.'

I don't think so, thought Gallaghan, not them, not at
the end. He asked, 'What did the preacher-man do?'

'He went out with the posse. He wanted the law to do
what had to be done.'

'He would. But it didn't work, did it?'

'Nope. And not long after that Burt Lucken had a
stroke. He's purty helpless I heard.'

'Tell me about this Rafe Tringle.'

'He comes here to Dodge sometimes. He comes here
to my place. He likes the whorehouse too. Cyprus End
ain't got much like that, not with the preacher-man
lookin' over it. I guess Lucken doesn't know what his
boy gets up to when he travels all the way to Dodge
City.'

'It figures,' said Gallaghan. 'Or does it?'

'You tell me. I guess Rafe left no stone unturned an'
crossed all his T's as well, huh?' said Buff, who had
heard most but not all of the story, a long, terrible,
convoluted one.

'I guess he figured Fat Brackley was after him,
coming all this way – blackmail maybe.'

'And the fat man only came to retire with his sister?'

'We'll never know whether that's the whole truth or
not maybe,' said Gallaghan.

'But you're here to find out if you can, an' to finish
it?'

'Like you say, if I can.'

But then Buff dropped his bombshell. 'Tonight is Rafe Tringle's night, his one night in the week, if he comes at all. He plays here first. Young Paul thinks he cheats. He don't stay till the small hours, though, Tringle don't. He's got a little whore down the street a piece.'

Gallaghan rose slowly and a little hesitantly. The end of it, he thought. Maybe tonight. But would it be the end, the *real* end? And if so, an end for whom?

'I did hear that Rafe's kinda sneaky with a gun,' Buff said.

Young Paul had been briefed. He said that the bespectacled Rafe kept a pistol in a shoulder holster, a real sneak gun. Paul didn't like guns like that, he said, but when Gallaghan asked him what kind of gun it was, he said he didn't know. One very hot night when Rafe was playing poker he'd taken off his fancy coat, then he'd taken the pistol out of its sneak holster and put it in the back of his belt. No, it wasn't a derringer, a mite bigger than that.

Paul said that at that time he hadn't seen a knife but he'd heard that Rafe carried a knife.

Buff said he'd heard that as well, that Rafe had gotten in a fight with a man in Cyprus End over a woman and had stuck him. Buff had heard that Rafe's boss, Lucken, rancher-cum-preacher-man, had had the wounded man fixed and well compensated.

He would, said Gallaghan.

Paul said he'd give the word if Rafe turned up.

Buff and his old friend, Gallaghan, talked about Cyprus End and the ranch, which was called the Triangle B and was owned by ex-preacher-man Burt Lucken who had made a mighty good thing of it, was a fine boss, loyal to his folk. Gallaghan asked about folks he remembered from the ranch. Buff said he figured some of the old hands would still be there. He asked Gallaghan if he remembered old Mose. Gallaghan said, yeh, he remembered Mose well, he'd been the sort of general factotum.

Still was, Buff affirmed to Gallaghan's surprise. Still spry so he'd heard, Buff said, nursed his boss, his old friend who was no longer able to look after himself right well.

Paul came in again to say that Rafe had turned up and taken a hand at a poker table. Gallaghan went back with the look-out into the main room and took a surreptitious look at his quarry, the young man with the eye-glasses that Fat Brackley had described.

Didn't look much.

But you never could tell . . . .

The young look-out man and his companion returned to the side of Buff. Paul had a drink before returning to his post. His stint wasn't yet finished.

He had already volunteered to go with Gallaghan at the end, back him up. But the big feller – gently, Buff had thought – had turned down the offer.

Paul had said that he knew the girl that Rafe visited late after a session at the tables. Rafe stayed over with this filly and left early the next morning in the little gig with the trotting horse he came in and stashed at the most convenient stables at the edge of town. Then, no doubt, he took the trail back to the Triangle B, maybe called in at the neighbouring strangely-named Cyprus End, maybe not.

# TWENTY

Gallaghan remembered the stand of old cottonwoods and wasn't surprised to find them still there. They had spread, were thicker. This was the way Rafe and his gig would come out of Dodge City. Mighty convenient.

Gallaghan drew Rip into the cover of the trees. The big bay was tractable, obviously entering into the spirit of the thing. It was all a game to him.

It was very early in the morning. Gallaghan hadn't watched the place where he knew Rafe was sleeping with his girl. It had been pointed out to him by Paul before the young man went to his own rest. The town slept. A lone man on the quiet street might have been spotted, though, so Gallaghan had ridden Rip slowly out of there as if for an early morning canter. The cottonwoods were just out of sight of the edge of town.

It was a benign morning with the sun slowly beaming. Shyly even, but with its warmth slowly growing. Unless things changed dramatically it was going to be a fine day.

Not a day on which to die.

It was cool in the shade of the cottonwoods and Gallaghan dismounted but kept the horse near him. Rip, sensing the waiting mood, cropped at the short grass and seemed to find it sweet.

But suddenly the horse raised his head, and his ears pricked. He had obviously heard something that his master had not yet noted.

Then Gallaghan heard a faint creaking.

Then the hiss of wheels on the hard beaten earth, the trail out of this side of town being pretty smooth.

He patted Rip's flank, and then climbed up into the saddle.

He waited for a small time before gentling the horse out into the middle of the trail.

Such a quiet end to a long, twisted and terrible trail.

With the horse and rider blocking his way, Rafe pulled the gig to a halt, the handsome little paint pony doing a restless little jig before settling, eyeing the bigger horse curiously.

Gallaghan drew his gun, levelled it at the bespectacled young man, said, 'Get down carefully. I have a message for you from Fat Brackley.'

Half a lie. But apt.

'Who in hell are you?' Rafe demanded. He had a querulous high-pitched voice.

I wonder if he knows who I am, Gallaghan wondered, and is playing for time. He didn't answer the question, said, 'Get down. Very carefully.'

Rafe started to get down, couldn't raise his hands at

the menace of the levelled Colt – his seat was high and he used both his hands; and he was very careful. As he hit the ground with his dainty feet in their high riding-boots, Gallaghan said to him, 'I'm gonna give you an even chance.'

And the big man holstered his gun.

Not till the last split second did Gallaghan realize that somehow, perhaps earlier even, Rafe had moved his pistol from its shoulder holster to the front of the ornate belt which showed beneath his open coat. The gleaming buckle. The gleaming, deadly-looking little gun.

By Gar, the bastard was fast! I should've got down, Gallaghan thought, twisting sideways in the saddle, reaching. The pistol sounded loud for so small a weapon! He felt a blow to his wrist. On the hand that held the gun but then couldn't seem to lift it. He lost his balance. He didn't pitch from the saddle but tumbled awkwardly from it and rolled in the dust and was suddenly able to pull the trigger in a sort of reflex action before the Colt dropped from his nerveless fingers.

The horse, Rip, had backed off. The paint at the gig looked startled but was also out of harm's way.

Both men were on the ground now. Gallaghan's slug had got Rafe in the shoulder. His pistol had paraboled in the air and hit the ground hard, being triggered accidentally, the slug whining away into nothingness, the flat echoes dying.

The wound in Gallaghan's right wrist poured blood but, rising into a crouch, he was seeing things clearly.

His gun had fallen behind him. Rafe was right in front. He had been hit in the left shoulder, had lost his pistol. His right hand went up and around to the back of his neck. A sneak knife, Gallaghan thought: he'd known folks before who kept a knife in that hidden place. He rolled sort of sideways reaching with his left hand for his own knife in the back of his belt. The heavy broad-bladed thing: a good *thrower*.

He threw it by the blade. In an underhanded way, watched it spin, gleam in the morning sun.

Rafe's knife was out, but went over his head and behind as Gallaghan's blade dug powerfully into his chest, pushing him backwards.

Gallaghan, half-crouching, moved towards him, his bleeding wrist held up against his chest, his other hand half bent in front of him, fingers held in a claw.

Rafe had already become stretched out as if he aimed to sleep.

His glasses had fallen from his nose and rested on his cheek. Gallaghan's knife protruded from the lean breast like some strange growth, embedded almost to the hilt, so powerful had been the throw.

The pale blue eyes, without the glasses covering them, were peacefully dead.

Gallaghan stooped and, with his left hand, drew out the knife. He bent to clean the gleaming red blade on Rafe's pants and then, almost unconsciously, changed his mind, wiped the weapon across the earth, ground it into the hard soil savagely before quickly stashing it in its old place.

He went back to his horse, his war-bag where he kept rudimentary medical supplies in a small wrap-around hold-all. He bandaged his wrist tightly, if bloodily. There was a jagged tear from the spinning bullet, but no bones had been touched, it seemed.

The horse, Rip, nuzzled him as if in commiseration.

It was very hot. The sun was brilliant and old Mose was looking into it. He pushed his glasses down his nose and shaded his eyes. He could see further then: that was the way his eyes were.

That was Rafe's gig all right, approaching. But that wasn't Rafe up there on the seat. It was a much bigger man.

Mose leaned forward. The trotting paint became clearer. Then the man. And he began to look kind of familiar.

Mose moved forward. The gig got nearer. The big man reined in the horse. The wheels ceased to spin. They stopped altogether.

'Lem Gallaghan,' Mose said.

'Mose, old friend. How are you?'

'I'm livin', boy, just livin'. What you doin' with Rafe's gig, Lem?'

'Rafe's dead. I left him with the undertaker in Cyprus End. Didn't figure to bring him any further.'

'Did you kill him, Lem?'

'Yes. He tried to kill me.' And that was the truth.

'It had to happen sooner or later I guess.'

156

'I've gotta see the boss, Mose. I heard how he is. But I've gotta talk to him.'

'I guess,' said the old man, bent, grey-whiskered. Always grey-whiskered as the young man remembered him.

Before Gallaghan could speak again, Mose went on: 'What happened to him has taken his speech. But not his faculties. Not that. Nor his eyes. He watches everything. And he can write. He's a good writer.'

'I remember,' said Gallaghan. 'He was always a good writer. The best of us all.'

'Hell,' said Mose. 'I cain't write anything more'n my own name – much. But I can talk.'

'Yeh, you allus could.'

'The boss writes me letters, y'know. An' though I cain't write back I can decipher the words. And he makes 'em simple. You ought to get down from that seat, Lem, and listen to me first. Make it like it used to be in the old days.'

Gallaghan didn't say anything then. He just got down. And they stood side by side near one wheel of the gig and Mose talked.

'Rafe got the money from the safe. He had the combination. The boss trusted 'im in everything. He paid those two killers to get the three bank robbers who were left, who'd killed Billy. He didn't tell the boss he'd done it till afterwards when it was too late for anybody to do anything about it. He said he did it for the boss. And for the boss's dead son who'd been like a brother to him. Maybe this was right.

'It was right by him I guess. He was a strange one. The boss would've wanted the law – an old preacher like him. He'd never really let go on that. Afterwards I guess he didn't know what to do, particularly after Rafe told him about the feller who got killed by mistake . . . .'

'My friend,' put in Gallaghan. He wondered whether Rafe had also told the boss about the knifing of Fat Brackley. He decided not to ask. Mose didn't mention it.

They walked to the house. The horse and gig were taken over by a young ranny and the visitor and his old companion went into the house.

It was twilight when Gallaghan left.

He had stayed over for a meal.

He took a memory with him of an old friend who sat in a high-backed armchair and listened to a story told by a visitor who had once been a sort of protégé of his. An old man who watched and listened with sad, intelligent eyes in a long weathered face that spoke of a suffering that couldn't now be actually voiced. An old man who then shakily wrote words on a white sheet of paper using a quill pen and a bottle of blue ink.

Words of forgiveness and understanding.

The words of the preacher-man.

As he left the ranch Gallaghan looked around him. He would make for another ranch now. A long way away.

Such a small ranch.

A ranch you could fit up in one corner of these

green and sprawling ranges and forget it was there.

But a ranch that Gallaghan would not exchange for twice the range of these rich holdings. A small ranch where a loving woman called Julie and a spirited boy called Jonathon awaited the return of a wanderer.